Kaitland Trevilian faces a dilemma.

"Kaitland."

The way he said her name sounded so helpless, pleading.

"Meet me here again. I'll send a message when I can arrange it. Please say yes."

She couldn't resist the entreaty in his voice and especially his eyes. She was nodding as she took the reins and prepared to mount. "All right, I'll try."

Christopher moved with lithe, muscular control to help her mount, but she was already in the saddle, riding away in a flurry. She soon questioned the prudence of her promise to him. The more involved she became, the more dangerous her position. Tomorrow she was to see General Johnston about what may very well be the largest campaign of the war, and she was becoming involved with a Federal officer. She no longer cared about gaining information from him. He was too clever for that anyway. Her only motive for seeing him again was purely personal. She hoped she did not live to regret the decision.

BONNIE L. CRANK lives in Virginia. *Another Time
. . .Another Place* marks Bonnie's debut with
Heartsong Presents.

Another Time. . .
Another Place

Bonnie L. Crank

Heartsong Presents

A note from the author:

DEDICATION
To my husband, Carlysle, with love. Your keen appreciation for Civil War history inspired this book. You were always there for me with support and patience, eager to share bits of information and facts to lend authenticity to the story.

ACKNOWLEDGMENT
With gratitude to my dear friend, Jean Crump, who encouraged and cheered me on. Your willingness to edit has been a priceless gift. Thanks for the laughter. . .

I love to hear from my readers! Write to me at the following address:

Bonnie L. Crank
Author Relations
P.O. Box 719
Uhrichsville, OH 44683

ISBN 1-55748-586-0

ANOTHER TIME. . .ANOTHER PLACE

one
Early Spring 1862

Gray clouds drifted across the inky sky, obscuring a three-quarter moon and plunging the stable into darkness. Acrid smoke from fires stoked in the main house and slave quarters stung her eyes and throat. If it were not for Kaitland's keen sense of direction and knowing the grounds like the back of her hand, she would have stumbled on the uneven path.

She carried no lantern for fear of alerting her father. Ethan Trevilian must never learn of his only daughter's involvement with the war effort. Poor Papa, she thought, pain flitting across her already troubled mind. As the cruel war raged on, more fiercely and much longer than anyone dreamed possible, the southern gentleman had slowly withdrawn from reality. The effects of war on his beloved southland and the gradual deterioration of Glen More had been too much for him. His enormous financial support of the Confederacy had placed the plantation in jeopardy, and now Kaitland was struggling to prevent the sale of part of the land.

The only sounds were those of courting frogs in a nearby pond and a chorus of crickets that seemed louder than usual to Kaitland's alerted senses. Blood pounded in her chest from a myriad of emotions. It would be necessary to draw on inner strengths to accomplish the dangerous task she faced tonight. If caught, she would be sent to prison . . . or worse.

Shuddering from a sudden chill, she made a conscious effort to push such disturbing thoughts from her mind. She could not remember a time when faith had not been part of her life; it was no less important during these trying times.

A gentle early spring breeze, fragrant with the first hint of honeysuckle, rustled the branches of the huge oak trees that lined the narrow path leading to the stables. It was a large structure, having housed many horses for the 4,000-acre plantation.

A sense of urgency spurred her on with the muted tread of her boots lost in the sounds of the night. She had disposed of the usual finery and fashionable equestrian habit and had chosen, instead, a pair of her father's buckskin trousers for easier mounting and riding. They were much too large for her, but a few alterations had rendered them the most practical attire for her purpose.

She smiled, remembering her boyish reflection in the full-length, gilt-framed mirror. She had carefully arranged her long, heavy red-gold mane in a neat chignon before pulling an old slouch hat low on her head. As she arranged her hair, the severe style began to add years to her youthful features, enhancing her beauty. Large green eyes, sooted with dark lashes were wide-set in a delicate heart-shaped face. A full sensuous mouth flattered her almost fragile bone structure and high cheekbones. She possessed an ethereal quality that complemented her petite, fully feminine figure, creating a mystique and complex air which had drawn many suitors from surrounding plantations and farms.

She had graciously declined several proposals of marriage, to her father's disappointment. By his rigid standards, she was fast approaching spinsterhood at the tender age of twenty-one.

Kaitland sighed in her moment of introspection. Marriage would have to wait. For her, love was the prerequisite to marriage and not how many acres a gentleman owned or if he was from a good family. With the war dragging on, most of the eligible bachelors had long since taken up arms. So many would never come home, she thought sadly.

"Is dat you, Miz Kaitlan'?" A thick, large black servant peered from inside the stable door, eyes wide with apprehension.

"Yes, Amos. Have you saddled Prince for me?"

The familiar, pungent smell of hay and manure filled Kaitland's nostrils as she brushed past the only person on the plantation who knew of her secret activities for the Confederacy. He was the most trusted man her father owned and had considered her safety his personal responsibility ever since her birth.

All of their workers had been devoted to her father, but since the war some had run off. Those who remained did so because their needs had always been met by Master Ethan, but this was becoming increasingly difficult considering their dwindling supplies and few hard-to-come-by replacements.

"Yes, 'um, but I prayin' you is decided to unsaddle dat devil hoss. He ain't no fittin' mount for a lady."

Amos stood near a low-burning lantern, anxiously turning a worn hat in his roughened, gnarled hands.

Kaitland smiled at the kindly old man. His short, stubby

hair had been gray for many years and the once youthful mahogany skin was now wrinkled and leathery. The eyes were still as she had always remembered them, caring and gentle. She had seen him supervising a hundred people in the fields and never had his authority been questioned. He could perform the work of three men, handle a runaway team, and in the next moment cradle, ever so gently, an infant in those calloused, massive hands. How could she ever manage without this faithful friend?

"Now, Amos, you know I've been riding since my first birthday. I can handle Prince. I need a swift, surefooted animal tonight. The patrol is downriver, but I'm not sure how far. I certainly don't want a horse that will give out or pull up lame."

Kaitland turned toward Prince's stall, but even in the dim lighting she glimpsed a shocked look on Amos' face. "Amos, what's wrong?" she asked, perplexed.

"Lausy, Miz Kaitlan', what is you awearin'?"

"Why, Papa's pants. They are much more practical than a cumbersome riding habit."

"What would your papa say, child? Dat ain't no way for a lady t' dress. You ain't never gone out o' here dressed in a such's dat before."

"I know, Amos, but skirts slow me down and so does the sidesaddle."

"Yes, 'um, and dats another thing. It ain't right you ridin' dat hoss astraddle. Now I knows why you said t' saddle dat hoss with your papa's saddle. You is gonna ride dat devel hoss astraddle," Amos said in disbelief, the whites of his eyes shining in the darkness.

Kaitland moved to stand in front her trusted friend, plac-

ing a hand over his. "It's all right. I'll be back before you
know it. Don't look so worried." Dwarfed in the shadow
of his towering frame, she attempted to project a calm she
did not feel.

"I does worry, Miz Kaitlan'. You bin like one o' my
very own ever since your mama died, and what you is fixin'
t' do is danjrus." A frown further creased his wrinkled
forehead and concern in the liquid black eyes reflected the
genuine misgivings he obviously had about this ride.

"Them riffraff Yankees is aroamin' all over da countryside now. No tellin' what they'll do if they gits their hands
on a perty young thing like you. 'Specly with a git-up like
dat. Now I knows you don't want t' hear what I'm sayin',
but I have t' speak my mind. This here spyin' business is
gonna cause you a peck o' grief."

Kaitland stepped back with hands on her hips. The determined set of her jaw and the fire in her emerald-green
eyes sparkling rebelliously left no doubt she would not be
deterred.

"Amos, not another word, do you hear me? This is one
way I can help the South, and I'm willing to take my chances
with Yankee soldiers. I'm tired of rolling bandages and
sewing uniforms."

Her voice rose stridently, but remorse quickly gripped
her heart as Amos' head slowly dropped, and it was plain
that she had wounded him deeply. Why did she always
speak before giving a thought to the consequences? Her
quick tongue had provoked her father's wrath more times
than she cared to remember.

"Yes, 'um," he said, barely audibly.

Kaitland moved quickly and threw her arms around the

old man's bulky body, burying her face in the rough material of his jacket.

"Oh, Amos, I'm sorry. I shouldn't have shouted at you. It's . . well, it's just something that I have to do. Please try to understand." When she looked up at him again, he was smiling, revealing strong white teeth that appeared even brighter against his dark skin.

"Yes, 'um, I 'spec it is, but dat don't make it easier t' watch you ride out o' here alone."

He took a deep breath and sighed heavily, letting the air out slowly, shaking his large head. "Well, if you is goin', I 'spec you best be on your way. Dat moon is back o' them clouds now, and you needs da dark."

Kaitland stepped back and smiled at the old gentleman, feeling contrite. "I would feel safer if there was no moon at all. Moonlight gives a sharpshooter the advantage, making me an easy target." Turning, she hurried to the impatient horse pawing the dirt floor in his stall.

"Easy, boy. You'll have a good run tonight," she crooned softly, stroking the handsome black stallion's massive head. His ears flicked forward as he gentled, responding to her soothing voice, sensing the challenge ahead. She had managed to keep him despite the financial condition of the plantation. He would bring a sizable sum on the market in Richmond, should she be forced to sell him.

"Now, Miz Kaitlan', did you have t' go an say somethin' about a sharpshooter? Lausy, child, you is takin' a terrible chance. Yes, 'um. A terrible chance." Amos spoke to himself, shaking his head while handing Kaitland the reins and helping her mount the huge animal.

"Yes, Amos," she murmured indulgently, smiling to herself. She had become accustomed to his ramblings.

He opened the stable doors and quickly glanced around the grounds. "It's all clear, Miz Kaitlan'," he whispered hoarsely.

Kaitland walked the anxious horse into the night air and slowly headed for the river. She turned to glimpse the silhouette of the main house. She might never see it again if anything went wrong tonight.

It was an impressive home with an imposing, magnificent portico. Monumental Doric columns had been added to the house in the 1850's when the Greek Revival temples had become popular in southern architecture. Numerous windows allowed floods of light to brighten their home. With its huge chimneys and large wings, the grandiose splendor of the mansion was complete. Kaitland especially loved the large fanlight in the wide gable on the third floor. As a child she had played in that room, sitting for hours gazing at the panoramic view afforded her from its height.

The house stood like a sentinel, a safe harbor where nothing could ever harm her. Then something had intruded into their comfortable way of life. Their traditions had epitomized the days of gentility, but the war had changed every aspect of their lives.

Convicted with a cause, she had chosen to do her part in a manner more daring and dangerous than sitting at home, wringing her hands. She was well aware women were considered subordinate in a male-dominated society, but it was of little consequence to her. Possessing a spirit and courage envied by her peers, she could do no less for the South she loved. There was a job to be done and she was going to do whatever she could—no matter the danger.

She had been forced to grow up at an early age by having to assume responsibilities as lady of the house. Since her mother's death, shortly after Kaitland's birth, her father had come to depend on her domestic managerial skills.

During her late teen years, talk of secession and war had filled every parlor throughout the South as the yeast of dissent fermented. She had been privy to many heated conversations between her father and neighboring landowners. It was not considered a woman's place to join in such discussions for they were looked upon as empty-headed pieces of fluff that could not fathom the intricate and delicate ways of politics. When would they learn that women, too, had brains capable of meeting challenges beyond the bedroom and the nursery?

If the truth were known, she thought, it was the women who were the backbone of the plantations and farms, managing them with their skills and proficiency. She had as much at stake in this war as anyone and she must do her part. Glen More would one day be hers. By listening attentively, though saying little during the discussions, she had learned a great deal about every facet of the war as the men saw it.

She was several yards from the stable before she urged her steed into a canter. It was impossible to break into a full gallop until she reached the river's edge and the clearing along the bank. The river was unusually low for this time of year, which fortunately left a wider shoreline to follow. She shivered, more from apprehension than from the cool, misty air and darkness that surrounded her like a shroud.

≈

Amos returned to the stable after Kaitland was out of sight.
He closed the doors, making his way to a soft bed in one of
the stalls. He was too concerned about her safety to leave
now, so he would wait here for her return and see to her
horse. There would be no sleep for him this night or any
other night when his mistress took it upon herself to win
the war single-handedly. Finding the hay very inviting, he
settled down to rest his weary old bones.

"Laud, you knows my hurtin' heart. Take care o' dat
foolish child. She's doin' what she reasons t' be right.
Don't make no difference if it be right or wrong, she ain't
never hurt nobody. Please, Laud, watch out for her. An',
Laud, if you ain't too busy, keep a hand on dat hoss. He's
a mean piece o' hoss flesh. Amen."

≈

Kaitland reached the river and turned Southeast, hoping
the patrol she sought was still in the area. Little Jesse, one
of her many informants, had reported seeing them biv-
ouacked near the old Ranson farm. He had been hunting,
waiting in a tree blind, when he spotted the patrol. True to
his promise to keep his eyes open for her, he reported to
her immediately . . . after he'd bagged his turkey.

To avoid suspicion, she simply told those who reported
to her she merely wanted to know how close soldiers came
to the main house. They found nothing unusual about her
interest in the movement of troops since her father's illness, for the complete responsibility of the plantation had
gradually fallen to her.

She smiled, dispelling the reflective mood, and brought
her attention back to the business at hand.

Murky-gray water lapped at the tree-lined shore, creating the illusion of a long, dark ribbon, rippling into the horizon. The wind, stronger on the water, whipped the trees into a frenzy of undulating arms that seemed intent on plucking her from her mount. The Chambray shirt she wore, plastered to her body like a second skin, tore loose from the buckskin trousers when she signaled the horse into a flat-out run, letting him have his head. She rode well, low in the saddle and close to the stallion's neck, experiencing the rare exhilaration she felt only when she was riding. She was given to carefree, reckless rides through the countryside, bareheaded, with her long hair blowing unfettered. Only then could she recapture the unburdened days of only a few years ago.

She had been brought up in a Christian home and believed in a Supreme Being and His concern for each soul on earth. The choice to become a spy for the Confederacy had led her into danger on more than one occasion, and she had come to know and feel His protective Hand.

Rounding a sharp bend in the river, Kaitland reined in her horse and gentled him to a stop, listening for any sound that might indicate the location of the patrol. If her information was correct, she was close to the area where she was told they would be.

Dismounting and walking quickly and quietly into the woods, she tied Prince to a tree and cautiously made her way through the low brush, ignoring the briars that picked at her trousers. Several horses whickered, sensing the closeness of another horse, and she moved in that direction.

Smoke from the dying embers of campfires filled the air and stung her eyes. About thirty yards from where she had entered the woods, eight horses were picketted. Beyond was a Confederate patrol camped for the night. It was difficult to see much more than the shadowy outline of the camp, but she could identify the First Virginia Infantry guidon leaning against a tree near the horses.

While trying to determine the best way to make her presence known without getting shot, the blood-chilling sound of a pistol being cocked at the base of her skull suspended her slightest movement. An inaudible gasp seemed to freeze in her lungs as night sounds became amplified, the blood pounding in her ears.

"Now jist raise them hands real slowlike and start walkin', mister."

The gruff voice from behind was low and menacing. It was all too apparent he would shoot first and ask questions later if she gave him the slightest provocation. Amos had been right about one thing; these clothes made riding easier, but she could be mistaken for a man in the dark.

It seemed prudent to follow her captor's instructions until she was certain this was Tim's outfit. She had known Tim Carrington for years, and he was with the First Infantry. She looked forward to seeing him again.

Kaitland raised her hands and started walking. She stepped around sleeping men on blankets as she was urged on her way to the only tent in the camp. Smoke from several campfires, mingled with lingering aromas from recently cooked food, drifted on the cool spring breeze. The only sounds were those of snoring men and an occasional whicker from the horses.

"That'll be far enough, fella'. Jist hold that position," the faceless voice from behind said impatiently as the cold steel of his pistol was pressed against her neck.

Kaitland trembled a bit, realizing the slightest movement could send her very swiftly to her Maker.

"Lieutenant, we got ourselves an intruder. You better come and see."

A faint glow illuminated the tent. They could hear the rustle of clothing hastily snatched amid sleepy grumblings from the occupant of the small shelter. The tent flap was thrown back, and a disheveled, tall blond man ambled through the opening, yawning and scratching a stubby beard of several days' growth.

"Corporal, this had better be good—what the? Kaitland?"

Holding the lantern higher and walking closer, a broad grin creased an otherwise very handsome, fatigue-lined face.

"Well, I'll be. Kaitland Trevilian. I heard you were passing information on to our men. I can't think of any other reason why you would be out here in the dead of night in that getup. For heaven's sake, put your hands down."

"Hello, Tim. How are you?"

He looked very much the same as she remembered him from the dance at his parents' home nearly a year ago. A little older and thinner, perhaps, and a great deal more weary, but still a handsome figure.

"You know this fel—excuse me, ma'am, but I sure thought you was a . . . I mean . . .," her captor said, stumbling over his words.

Kaitland had nearly forgotten about the man until his words tumbled out and she saw him for the first time. Poor man. He was so shocked and embarrassed she felt compelled to relieve his misery.

"It's all right, Corporal," she said sympathetically. "I admit this is a bit unorthodox, but it affords easier traveling."

"Yes, ma'am," he said uncomfortably, pulling his cap from a balding head.

"That will be all, Corporal," Tim said curtly.

"Yes, sir." The soldier saluted crisply and disappeared as quickly as he had appeared behind Kaitland in the woods.

Kaitland's attention was drawn to Tim's sudden, intense scrutiny of her. She could almost feel the sweep of emotion that animated his features. There was a warmth in his eyes that made her feel special as he moved to stand in front of her.

"You're as beautiful as I remember." His voice was low and soft, like a caress. "But," he said sighing, "I'm certain this isn't a social call. I was right, wasn't I? You've heard or seen something that could help us."

"Yes, I think this is significant." Relieved that he had directed his thoughts to the reason for her being there, she was anxious to relate the information gleaned from her informant. The war was taking a nasty turn and they needed every scrap of intelligence they could gather. Richmond had become the Union's next target.

"Come and sit, Kaitland. You've had a long ride. How did you ever convince your daddy to let you spy?"

"No. There isn't time to sit. I must get back before I'm missed or run into an early morning Yankee patrol. Papa is—" She thought of her father and his declining health. her eyes misted as she lowered her lashes, not wanting Tim to see her anxiety. "Papa doesn't know about . . .

well, I haven't told him about my activities, and he mustn't find out."

Tim raised his brows and released a slow, modulated whistle, rolling his eyes toward the night sky. "I wouldn't want to be in your shoes when he finds out. Why he—"

"I haven't time to discuss my father," she said sharply, cutting him off.

"I'm sorry, Kaitland. I didn't mean to upset you."

She could understand his appraising glance. It was not like her to be so short tempered. But he was a very astute man, and she felt certain he would figure out why she had to keep her undercover work for the Confederacy a secret. News of her father's condition had already traveled through-out a tri-county area, and Tim was sure to hear of it from his parents' letters.

Tim cleared his throat and continued. "You mentioned Yankee patrols. Have you seen them?"

"No, but one of my sources has about ten miles west of Glen More."

"That doesn't sound good," he said nervously, running his fingers through the tousled shock of hair.

"Tim, how long have you been on the river?"

"Just a few days. Why do you ask?" Uneasy curiosity crept into his eyes as he frowned.

"Then you haven't seen the Union patrol boats scouting the area?"

"Lord, no. Have you seen them?" His voice was heavy with anxiety as he stepped closer to her. "I've heard ru-mors about an amphibian invasion, but no one knows for sure if it's so or which waterway they'd use. McClellan controls the inland waters, but he could just as well use the

James or the York River to attack Richmond. Those Yankees took a beating at Bull Run, but you can bet they're getting ready for something big." He spoke half to himself as though thinking out loud, turning all possibilities over in his mind.

He took her by the shoulders, peering deeply into her eyes. "You took a tremendous risk coming here tonight. The Confederacy is in your debt. I'll get this information back to my commanding officer by dispatch immediately."

His hands tightened on her arms, and he moved closer, his warm breath feathery on her face. "You know how I have always felt about you ... I ... you never gave me a chance to tell you, to explain—"

"We can't think of ourselves now. We both have a job to do. There is so much death and destruction around us. We have to think of the South first," she murmured pleadingly.

She was well aware of Tim's feelings, but she had always considered him a friend and nothing more. Encouraging him now would only hurt him later.

Dropping his hands, Tim straightened his tall frame, closing his eyes briefly, as if to banish the logic of her words. "You're right, of course. 'Thank you' seems inadequate in light of what you have done, but let's hope your reward will be in the South's victory and a swift end to this madness." His intonation was firm but resigned.

"Thanks, Tim. I'll leave now. I must get home before dawn," she said, taking his hands in hers and forcing a lightness to her voice. The longing in his eyes made her question her sense of justice. It seemed so wrong to hurt him this way, but worse to pretend feelings she didn't possess. He was too much a man to settle for brotherly affection and that was all she could offer.

"Take care."

"Good-bye, Kaitland. Please be careful."

She made her way back to Prince, still tethered in the woods. She thought about the years she had know Tim and the hours they had spent together as children. Of all the young men who had attempted to attract her attention, he was the only one she wished she could truly care for.

Her father had attributed her lack of interest in the many eligible callers at Glen More to her daring, free spirit. He felt she would settle down when the time came. She had often wondered what magical spell would take place when the time came. For several years her father had laughed it off and said jovially that she was exactly like her mother. It delighted him to see so many characteristics of his Adeline in his daughter. For many months, however, before his illness had taken a more serious turn, he had encouraged her to select a young man who could take care of her when he was gone.

The same rough voice from nowhere it seemed, rumbled through the still night air. Kaitland jumped, a sudden lump of fear in her throat. She was plummeted back to the realities of the present.

"I'll walk you to the river, ma'am. I'm real sorry about the way I treated you before."

Kaitland exhaled a sigh of relief. "Corporal, you nearly scared me out of ten-years' growth."

"Sorry, ma'am, but I jist want t' see you're okay as far as I can go."

"Thank you, Corporal, but I can manage. The real danger is beyond here." She untied her horse and turned toward the river.

"Ma'am?"

She stopped and turned. "Yes, Corporal."

"Sure is nice to have made your acquaintance." The shabbily dressed soldier brought himself to full attention and proudly saluted her. Few of the enlisted men were fortunate enough to have regular army uniforms. The average rank and file wore what they had brought with them from home, having acquired few army-issue items.

"What's your name, Corporal?"

"Why, it's Toby Beamer, ma'am," he said, his hard features breaking into a boyish grin.

"Godspeed, Toby Beamer."

Then she slipped into the darkness and everpresent dangers.

two

Low ground fog swallowed Kaitland, the mist cool upon her face. The atmosphere on the river had changed in the early morning hours as dawn approached. A stillness, almost tangible, spawned an eerie cloak of dread and expectancy. It seemed the entire world was poised, ready for—what?

Kaitland shook herself and mounted the anxious horse, eager to recapture the freedom of racing an unobstructed track. She must not tarry in the few hours remaining before the eastern sky brightened with the charcoal gray light of dawn.

Spurring Prince into action, she tensed the muscles of her legs to gain a comfortable riding position. She had acquired her equestrian skills from her father's vast knowledge of horses. Racing horses had been his weakness, and Prince was the only thoroughbred left from a long line of racing stock, the result of many years of careful breeding. This fact and her father's health had convinced her to keep the animal. She felt that seeing his favorite horse might help to ease his troubled mind.

Kaitland's attention was suddenly drawn to a movement on the river. She quickly reined in her horse and led him into a wooded area where she dismounted and stealthily hid in some tall brush.

Weakness invaded her limbs as she crouched low,

straining to pierce the darkness. Not too far in the distance she saw the outline of a vessel heading her way. The moon, still concealed behind thick clouds, was low in the sky, but enough illumination broke through to reveal a dreaded Federal gunboat. Her breath caught in her lungs, so breathing became difficult, almost painful. The only possible reason for their presence would be to scout the James River as a feasible invasion route.

The ghostly vessel moved easily downstream, steam belching from its stack. It seemed an eternity, and still it had not reached the stretch of water where Kaitland crouched, watching and waiting; then she realized why. They were stopping in midstream to lower a rowboat.

Fear surged through every fiber of her body. Her skin prickled and blood pounded in her head. They were sending a scouting party ashore. If she were caught, prison would be a certainty.

There was nothing to do except to leave the easier riverbank path and travel inland. It would slow her down and take much longer, but she had no choice. All she would need now was to run into a Yankee patrol.

Prince was not happy about the change in plans. He snorted and reared his massive head to express his displeasure, but her soothing encouragement finally settled him. He seemed to sense the danger and the consuming fear that held his rider in its cold grip.

Making her way cautiously through the woods, she thought she had ridden far enough from the gunboat to relax. The scouting party was making its way on foot. She was sure they were unaware of her presence. They had not been on land long enough to discover her.

Weary of body and spirit, she longed for the soft downy comfort of her bed. She had not slept well the previous night, and this long ride was taking its toll on her strength.

How could she think only of herself when their men in uniform suffered such trials on the battlefield? Straightening her back to ease the tension, she berated herself for complaining. Some battle-worn soldiers were going for days without sleep, with low rations, marching through all kinds of weather and adverse conditions, and still they fought on.

She stopped at an old logging road that led to the river, but to take it would mean traveling in the open. She needed to be certain it was deserted before crossing; however, to do so was to face the threat of exposure.

In the distance she heard the rhythmic sound of horses' hooves. Though she was well hidden in the trees, she was concerned about Prince. He could easily give away her presence. She dismounted and rubbed the horse's nose, murmuring softly into his ear. Would this night never end?

Gradually the galloping horses grew nearer, their hoofbeats growing louder and louder until the ground vibrated beneath her. A Union patrol passed within yards. As the last man passed from view, Prince neighed and pulled away from her grasp. She caught the reins and held him fast, but the patrol had been alerted and ordered to stop.

"Sergeant, check those woods," said a deep, authoritative voice.

"Yes, sir. Jones, Corky, Jamison, follow me."

Kaitland had already mounted and was urging her horse into the dense forest. Her knowledge of the land and her swift horse were her only advantages.

"There he goes, Lieutenant! Want us to run him down?"

The excited shout pierced Kaitland's mind as she blended into the night.

"No, we'll lose him in these woods. It's still too dark. He probably knows his way around in these parts like a fox. We'll check the plantations in this area."

"Yes, sir. We didn't see much though. What will we look for?" said the baffled sergeant.

"We will circle back to the main road and ride for the first farm on the river. Search for a horse that has been ridden hard. He may well be the spy we've been ordered to find. Move 'em out, Sergeant."

"Yes, sir. Column Left!" The patrol was signaled and they turned their mounts to follow the new directive.

"Gallop!"

Kaitland raced as fast as she dared, branches tearing at her clothes. Several hairpins loosened and flew from her hair, the long swath cascading down her back, the old hat lost during her frantic efforts to escape.

She road as if the very devil were after her. Where the Yankees were concerned, she wasn't sure that wasn't true. She had known fear many times while spying for the Confederacy, but tonight she was panic-stricken. This had been the closest she had ever come to being caught.

The capable horse made his way through the brambles and brush with agility and confidence. After jumping a small stream, Kaitland knew she was near Glen More. A few more moments and she entered the clearing just below recently plowed cornfields. The fragrance of freshly turned earth mingling with the smells of early morning filled and stimulated her heightened senses. She breathed deeply of the familiar scents, releasing a long sigh of relief and accomplishment. She was safe.

Amos opened the stable doors and yawned as Kaitland quickly dismounted, handing the reins to the tired old man.

"Is you all right, Mis Kaitland?" he asked sleepily, rubbing his black eyes with large knuckles.

"Yes, I'm fine, but a patrol will probably show up here shortly. Now don't forget, Amos, you know nothing." Her tone held a note of warning, and he nodded, eyes suddenly opening wide.

"Yankees? Laudy, Miz Kaitland, you best git t' da house. Them Yankees'll be snoopin' around here like a bunch o' bloodhounds."

"Just take care of Prince. I'll be fine. Now hurry," she coaxed, turning him around and giving him a gentle push.

"Yes, 'um. I goin'."

Kaitland rushed toward the house, noticing the first gray streaks of dawn filtering through the thick canopy of trees. Dew lay heavy on the soft grass, dampening her boots. She loved the dawn. It was her favorite time of day, but this was hardly the time to commune with nature.

Quickly, she crept through the stately house and climbed the wide, carpeted staircase to her room. Once inside she quietly closed the door and leaned against it. She needed a few more seconds to catch her breath and to calm her nerves before getting ready for bed. She must appear as though she had spent the night in her room.

A mental image of a bumbling Yankee patrol floundering through unfamiliar territory in the darkness drew a small, satisfied giggle from deep in her throat. No. They would probably take the longer route, if, in fact, they were coming at all.

A touch of fragrant lavender lingered in the warm room, drawing her into her world of safety, her own private sanctuary, her place of reprieve and rest. The large, canopied bed beckoned, but she was still much too edgy and alert to rest yet.

Light filtered through the windows with the shadowy fingers of dawn, and she uttered a small prayer of thanksgiving that she had returned unscathed. Peace and calm gradually replaced stress, and a stillness slowly settled over her trembling body. Her mission had been completed.

She loved her room, from the beautiful oak floors to the white ceilings and walls, the doors and windows graced with delicately carved pediments, simple and elegant. The large stone fireplace, flanked by two wing chairs, was her favorite place during the long, cold Virginia winters.

A heavy oak bed dominated the room with its exquisite hangings, curtains, and upholstery all of the same lovely fabric. The bed and accessories had been a gift from her father for her sixteenth birthday. She had spent hours in Richmond looking at fabric, finally selecting a delicate, yellow-flowered pattern with a beige-and-chocolate brown background.

A tiny rosewood desk, which had belonged to her mother, stood near one of three dormer windows. She cherished the desk as she did everything that had belonged to a mother she had never known.

Blinking several times, she reluctantly returned to the present and started peeling away the damp clothes. She poured water from the china pitcher into its matching basin. The cool water refreshed her flushed skin and soothed her sagging spirit. It had been a long night filled with terror, and her nerves were tightly strung. A feeling of disquiet that was never quite dispelled these days ebbed from her tired being.

The soft, pale pink batiste nightgown billowed around her ankles, falling over her graceful curves. She methodically brushed her long tresses with an inlaid mother-of-pearl hairbrush that had been a wedding gift from her father to his young bride years ago. The silky strands shimmered and snapped with each stroke.

The sound of approaching horses halted her hand in midair. She hastily donned the matching wrapper to her gown as her heart pounded in her breast. It had to be the Union patrol. No one else would visit Glen More at this early hour. How had they got here so quickly?

Kaitland rushed to the window, her hand convulsively touching her throat. Her worst fears had been realized. Coming through the gates at the entrance of their plantation was a Union patrol. Warily she watched the hated blue uniformed men advance on the dusty approach to the main house, but her eyes were drawn to the lieutenant commanding the detachment. He was a mountain of a man who rode straight and confidently. The distance prevented any clear discernment of his features, but it was evident by his bearing that he commanded with dignity.

With trembling hands, Kaitland secured her wrapper in place and lifted it just above her ankles as she charged down the stairs to the front hall. She fervently prayed this matter could be dispensed rapidly without disturbing her father.

Descending the last step, she nearly collided with Dulcie,

the maid. The rotund black servant was Amos' wife of
many years, and she had cared for the family since
Kaitland's birth. The poor thing was easily excited, and it
was apparent from her agitated state, that she, too, had
seen the patrol.

"Miz Kaitland, is you seen 'um? They is comin' right t'
da front door!" Eyes wide with fear and twisting her white,
stiffly starched apron mercilessly, she stood first on one
foot, then the other.

"Yes, Dulcie. I've seen them. Calm down. They won't
harm us, and I don't want to waken Father. Now open the
door."

"Lausy me, Miz Kaitland, you ain't gonna let 'um in, is
you? Dem Yankees got no manners a'tall," she said, her
voice growing louder. "Your papa should be here."

"Shhh! I don't want my father to hear this. He couldn't
handle it, Dulcie. You know his condition. Now do as I
say. Perhaps they will recognize simple courtesy."

Kaitland's words rang with confidence, but she was not
at all certain they would not be harmed. She was grateful
her father's room was on the second floor at the rear of the
house.

"I ain't so sure 'bout—"

"Dulcie!" The warning tone in Kaitland's voice was
enough to turn the old woman toward the door.

"Yes, 'um. I goin', but I don't likes it. No, 'um, I don't
likes it a'tall,' she said, opening the door cautiously as if a
great monster lurked on the other side.

The patrol had already stopped in front of the house.
The saddled soldiers sat with their Spencer rifles drawn,
the gun butts resting on their thighs. The tall lieutenant

had dismounted and was agilely ascending the steps.

A wide veranda, which stretched across the entire front of the house, afforded Kaitland an appraising view of the soldier as he easily covered the distance with long strides. This was no bumbling officer. There was little evidence of the hours he must have spent in the saddle for his dark blue uniform was impeccable from the short, belted jacket to his knee-high black Wellington boots. The yellow shoulder patches, collar, and trouser stripe identified him as a cavalry man. He wore the rank insignia of a lieutenant.

"I would like to see the master of the house, please," said the deep voice, shattering the morning calm.

"Da mas'r is still asleep an—"

"I'll take care of it, Dulcie," Kaitland said, stepping forward boldly, facing the stranger.

"I'm Kaitland Trevilian, Lieutenant. My father isn't well. Perhaps I can be of some assistance."

Kaitland's blood raced in her veins, pounding against her temples. He was so compellingly masculine. She did her best to ignore it, but the sheer size of this man would command anyone's attention. She could not draw her eyes away from his. They were intense and so intriguing she felt swallowed up in the deep brown, fathomless depths. His long, thick black lashes would have been envied by half the women she knew who lamented their short, stubby tufts.

"I'm Lieutenant Christopher Donovan with the Twenty-Seventh New York Cavalry," he said, removing his jauntily worn wide-brimmed hat with a gauntleted hand, "and I must inform you I have ordered my men to search the grounds. I trust you will have no objections."

His eyes had not left hers. The conversation seemed secondary, routine, while their true thoughts were left unspoken. There was a ruggedness about him, yet a gentleness beneath the surface that surrounded and held her. With deep-set eyes, a classically straight nose, and lips well defined, his features appeared to have been chiseled from granite. The masculine force of him was incredibly overpowering.

"Whatever for, Lieutenant? We are hiding nothing. The war hasn't reached us yet," she said in her prettiest southern drawl.

"The war has reached everyone in one way or another, ma'am." There was a challenge in his voice, still, he held her captive with the intensity of his gaze.

"I simply meant the fighting hasn't reached us, but you're quite right, the war has touched us all. Of course, search all you like, Lieutenant. May I inquire about the subject of your search?"

"We're looking for a Confederate informant. We have reason to believe there is one in this area. My patrol spotted a suspicious figure in the woods near here before dawn. We think he came in this direction."

She knew he was watching her carefully for the slightest hint in her expression that would indicate her knowledge of or involvement in spying for the Confederacy.

"Is there anyone else in the house?" For the first time he broke eye contact with her and nodded toward the interior of the house.

"Just my father, as Dulcie mentioned, but he has not been well and rarely leaves the plantation. The war has—" Her voice broke as she lowered her lashes, dropping her regard to the polished oak floor.

"I'm sorry." The sympathetic statement, barely above a whisper, conveyed a silent message more meaningful than words.

Kaitland raised her eyes and was once again drawn into this man's dark, penetrating scrutiny of her. It was evident he was genuinely sorry about her father. Momentarily, the stern military mask slipped and a gentle man surfaced to communicate empathy, one human being to another. The fact they were political enemies held no meaning for a moment. He seemed to be aware of what she was thinking and feeling. That didn't surprise her. In the strong male lines of his face, she detected experience with life and women.

What was happening to her? She had never reacted to a man like this before. This is nonsense. She didn't know him; and he was, of all things, a northerner.

Then there was an abrupt change of mood. He withdrew from the impassioned moment and stepped back, the military mask once again in place. It was as though he had been taken off guard just long enough to become himself and then had quickly snapped back into his role.

"We'll search the grounds first, and then I must ask you to allow a search of the house."

From the tone of his voice the request sounded more like a harsh command to her. She straightened her small frame and lifting her chin she nodded curtly, spun around on one heel and fled up the stairs. *Two can play that game, Mister Yankee Lieutenant,* she thought, resentment flaring through her. She must still her thudding heart and regain a semblance of composure before the officer and his men invaded the house. It would be less than desirable for the lieutenant to sense her hostility. She must present the appearance of complete compliance with his requests to avert suspicion from her.

Kaitland endeavored to clear her mind of what could happen when the soldiers entered their home. Looting, deliberate and willful destruction, or—no she couldn't think about that.

Entering her room, she hurriedly began to dress, when her eyes fell on the soiled, damp clothes worn during the dangerous night ride, a dead giveaway of her activities. Frantically, she gathered the clothes and stuffed them into the bottom of her trunk, carefully arranging extra linens and personal items on top. They were looking for a man, not men's clothing in a lady's trunk. Surely, even Yankees would conduct a discriminating search and not violate a woman's personal belongings.

Hastily rummaging through an assortment of day dresses, she chose a pretty moss green, two-flounce skirt trimmed with black braid and a wide grosgrain ribbon sash, caught up in poufs. The stiffly-boned bodice was designed as a separate piece with full split sleeves revealing a soft white blouse underneath. A crisp white collar and broach put the finishing touches on the stylish attire. Green was a complementary color for Kaitland, enhancing her eyes and accenting the red in her hair.

There was no time to arrange her hair, so she tied it back with a matching grosgrain ribbon. One last glance in the mirror reflected flushed cheeks and eyes much too bright for the innocence she must project. Was the heightened color a result of the harrowing night and the resulting search, or the tall, dark man she had just met?

From the vantage point of the front porch, she could view the meticulous search of several dependencies on the east side of the house. She found herself seeking out the handsome lieutenant as he directed the quest. She wondered if he would allow his men to steal whatever supplies they wanted. Conscience was not their forte.

Suddenly, a soldier came into view leading Prince. A strangled breath caught in her constricted throat. Not Prince. She could not let them take him. Considering her father's condition, she had, for all practical purposes, run the plantation for the past year, It was her responsibility to protect their property. She must at least make the effort to stop them.

It would have been proper for a lady of her station to approach the situation by walking demurely across the lawn with gown raised to a respectable length, affording small dainty steps. Not Kaitland. A serious problem required swiftly executed action. She raised her hooped skirt above her shins, the fullness billowing around her, and ran as gracefully as a young doe.

"Please, Lieutenant, leave Prince here. He means so much to my father," she said breathlessly.

It galled her to beg a Yankee, but if that is what it took, she would gladly get down on her knees.

She saw the smile that tugged at the corners of the officer's mouth as his gaze lingered on the curve of her shoulders and the tiny cinched waist of her fashionable dress. His measuring look had not missed an inch of the vision she created yet it was not offensive. She could imagine what he was thinking about her dash across the lawn. Clearing his throat, he raised his eyebrows and spoke in a well-trained military manner.

"Is this your father's horse?"

Kaitland was seized with the uneasy feeling there was more on his mind than the horse's ownership. "Yes, Prince is the last of his racing stock, and I've managed to keep him, hoping to ease my father's state of mind. Knowing his favorite stallion is still at Glen More gives him a great deal of pleasure."

"Miss Trevilian, this animal has been ridden hard very recently. How do you account for that?" he said pointedly, his eyes boring into hers, studying her reaction.

If ever she needed to be convincing, now was the time. "Why, I can't, Lieutenant, but I can assure you my father hasn't been out of the house all night."

Could he read her eyes? Could he sense the deception? She had come to realize in this brief acquaintance that he was a very discerning man and probably a good judge of character. Even in this critical moment, his nearness affected her so strangely. She was receiving signals from her body that until now were completely foreign to her. What was happening to her?

"There seems to be a number of unanswered questions here, but without more evidence than a tired horse, my hands are tied. My investigation, however, is far from over."

The cryptic remark hit Kaitland like a physical blow. Their plantation would no doubt be watched now, and that would seriously jeopardize her covert activities. It would be dangerous, but on the other hand, it might serve as a distinct advantage. She would be in a position to possibly gain more useful information. Lieutenant Donovan was no fool. She would have to be careful.

"Lieutenant, he sure would make a good replacement for the sorry mount I have now. I think I'll just take him." The sergeant who was holding Prince's bridle spoke for the first time and turned to leave, obviously assuming Kaitland's request would be denied.

"Sergeant, put that horse back in the stable." The stern order was given with menacing firmness, his intent clear.

"But, Lieutenant, we're supposed to put down the Confederacy. Leaving an animal like this—"

"Precisely," the officer said harshly, "our job is to cripple the Confederacy, not terrorize women and old men. Now, carry out my order, Sergeant."

"Yes, sir." The reprimanded soldier's face turned scarlet. His mouth shut with a snap, and an angry frown creased his brow.

Christopher Donovan turned to Kaitland. "I'm sorry, Miss Trevilian. I'm afraid some of our troops take unfair advantage of civilians. Your father's horse will remain his personal property."

"Thank you, Lieutenant," she whispered, a slow heat rising to flush her cheekbones.

Seconds, minutes, hours, days passed. Time stood still in the cool, fragrant, early morning mist beneath an old gnarled oak tree. In the midst of war, two political foes responded to an unspoken truce and simply became a man and a woman. The ancient attraction, as old as man, was profound and poignant, felt by both.

"Kaitland, I wish," he said, his dark eyes searching her face. The tightly controlled restraint was weakening, and he swayed almost imperceptibly toward her. He raised his hand and tentatively touched a tiny red-gold ringlet of her hair that curled softly at her temple.

She stood transfixed, held as if by gentle hands intent on keeping her a willing prisoner. The use of her given name after such a brief acquaintance would normally have offended her. Somehow it seemed so right when he said it. She liked the way it sounded.

He shook his head as if to clear it, then faltered. The moment was lost.

"Lieutenant, the men haven't found anything except that horse. That just leaves the house." The sergeant who had tried to take Prince studied his commanding officer as he approached the couple.

"Very well, Sergeant. I'll be right there. Assemble the men at the porch steps," he said in a clipped reply, his eyes still on Kaitland.

"Yes, sir."

"Miss Trevilian, I would prefer your presence during the house search. It is not my intention to frighten you," he said softly, his dark eyes saying so much more.

"I'm not frightened, Lieutenant. As I've said, we have nothing to hide."

A stab of guilt pierced her. The lie was becoming so natural, so easy to say. But she reminded herself that it was for the cause. Guilt was a voracious enemy. It was necessary to justify her undercover activities for the South, but was she compromising her principles by rationalizing? She could not dwell on that now. Here she was, not two hours after a mission for the Confederacy, declaring her innocence to a Union officer who was looking at her in such a way that made her knees tremble with weakness.

"Yes, you did say that, but . . ." His voice faded, and a strange resignation invaded his expression.

Kaitland felt the first flood of fear as she watched his

eyes become hooded and he looked away from her toward the house. Did he suspect? Her head began to pound, barely cognizant of his words. She clasped her perspiring hands together, willing her numb mind to continue playing the role.

"Perhaps we could get started." Turning abruptly, he offered Kaitland his arm, and they crossed the wide expanse of lush lawn to the porch where the patrol lazed about awaiting orders.

She watched the small command come to partial attention as they approached. The look on their faces gave evidence to their thoughts on Lieutenant Donovan's gallant attention to her. She overheard their whispered remarks and raucous laughter, and wondered how the officer at her side would accept such behavior.

Kaitland was aware of the sudden stiffening of his spine as she felt the muscles in his arm tense, becoming ridgid. Anger was apparent in his bearing and expression.

"Sergeant, I suggest you maintain a modicum of discipline and order among the men, or we'll find someone who can. Is that clear?"

His face wore a forbidding frown, leaving little room for doubt that he would have no compunction in carrying out the edict. The men fell silent and snapped to full attention.

"Yes, sir. It's very clear, sir. We're sorry for the outburst." The sergeant sobered, his face becoming an expressionless mask.

"Very well. Divide the men into teams. I want a systematic search."

"Yes, sir."

"And, Sergeant, there will be nothing disturbed except what is necessary for an orderly investigation. The men will not remove so much as a napkin from this house," he said with unbrookable firmness."

"Ah . . . yes, sir. I'll see to it."

The salute was stiff while the sergeant stood ramrod straight. His bearded face was still remarkably impassive, but Kaitland noted a hint of admiration flicker in his hazel eyes. Lieutenant Donovan was obviously a hard taskmaster, but his men respected him.

As they dispersed, the lieutenant turned to her, taking her elbow in his firm, warm grasp. She breathed in the clean, vital masculinity of this stranger. Ascending the steps, she became aware of his superior height and strength. Solid and sure of himself, she knew he would be a knight in shining armor for some lucky woman, and she found herself leaning into his protective vitality. It had been so long since there had been anyone upon whom she could lean.

"I hope you will forgive my men. They are loyal soldiers, but sometimes they forget their manners. Behind my back they refer to me as by-the-book Donovan. I have a feeling they are curious about my . . . shall we say, slight deviation from military procedure." He looked down at her and smiled.

Kaitland looked away, nervously fingering the folds of her skirt. It was unsettling to realize the soldiers in her house had observed their silent exchange moments ago. Had it been so obvious?

"I'm sorry. I've embarrassed you," he said when she couldn't bring herself to speak. "I didn't mean to."

"No," she said simply. "Don't be sorry. There's really nothing to apologize for."

He drew in a deep, audible breath as they entered the

mansion. "Perhaps you should see to your father before my men enter his room. Would it help if I accompanied you? I could explain."

"No, Lieutenant. It's best if I see him first. I'll send for Amos. He represents a time from the past where Papa lives now. Do you think it might be possible to take him to a room that has been searched and avoid contact with your men? You see, the uniform . . ." She hesitated, her eyes pleading for yet another concession. She felt the heat rushing to her cheeks as his eyes met hers. Although his gaze was unreadable, she thought she saw a flare of concern.

"Of course. I'll see to it while you summon whomever you need."

"Thank you, Lieutenant. You're very kind." Turning to find Amos, she could feel his eyes on her as she left the foyer. The sensation was akin to a physical touch that sent tingling waves washing through every nerve in her body.

"Miss Trevilian."

The deep, resonant tones of his voice excited her more than she cared to admit. "Yes," she said, half turning.

"Do you think it would be proper for a southern lady to address a Union officer by his given name?" The corners of his eyes creased and their depths twinkled with amusement. He watched as even, white teeth nibbled at her lower lip.

She could feel her flushed cheeks begin to burn with a sensation she could not identify. In those few seconds they had exchanged something. A promise? A secret? They had shared something indefinable and they both knew it. If they never saw each other after today, she sensed a special bonding had taken place.

Finding her voice, she said, "I doubt that it would be a

breach of the Articles of War, Christopher."

Smiling, she hurried away. His name sounded delicious. "Christopher," she whispered to herself, rolling the letters around her tongue. If they became friendly, perhaps, just perhaps she could learn some useful information about the Union's movements. Another deception. Why did he have to be so handsome? She groaned inwardly. Would this war never end?

※

Standing rooted to the floor, Christopher watched her trim, perfect figure recede through the door, wondering in amazement at the phenomenal fascination. It was more than fascination he felt for this beautiful, valiant young woman. Could she possibly know something about the shadowy figure in the woods this morning? He sincerely hoped not. How could he arrest that lovely creature? The Rebels had been one jump ahead of them too often for mere coincidence. There had to be an informant and the word circulating through command indicated they suspected a woman. The thought of her in prison turned his blood cold. There was intelligence in her pretty face, and from what he had seen, she managed this huge plantation with skill and deftness. If she knew more than she was telling, he might obtain information by staying close to the area. Those were his orders. Stay in the area, find and arrest the spy.

He squared his shoulders and released a deep, troubled sigh. The task of searching this house was not something he looked forward to. Sometimes he hated his job.

three

"Miz Kaitland, I ain't so sure your papa goin' with me. He gonna ask why, and I ain't got no answer."

Amos shuffled along behind Kaitland to her father's room. The first floor had been searched, and Christopher held his men in the back of the house until she moved her father to his study on the first floor. He seldom went there anymore, but she hoped to lure him under the pretext of helping her with the ledgers.

"Amos, just follow my lead. Papa has finished breakfast and will be coming downstairs soon. We must encourage him to help me in the study. I don't want to think about his reaction if he sees Union soldiers in his house."

Kaitland hastened to her father's room followed by the faithful servant. She fervently prayed this little guise would work.

"Yes, 'um. I try. Da mas'r sure don't need no more upsettin'."

She knocked softly on the solid walnut door and opened it, peeking in. "Papa, may I come in?"

"Of course, child. Come in." The timbre of Ethan Trevilian's voice, still strong and deep despite his advancing years, rang from the sitting room adjoining his bedchamber.

Kaitland swept into the room with exuberance, hoping to hide the shadows under her eyes from the sleepless night,

42

resorting to a little female fluttering. Her father might be failing, but he missed virtually nothing where she was concerned. In a flurry, she crossed the room and stood smiling before the aging gentleman, schooling her expression to reflect that nothing was amiss.

The master of Glen More was a large man with a full head of wavy gray hair. The neatly trimmed mustache and muttonchops added an air of dignity to his handsome leonine appearance. He wore a finely tailored dark suit with matching vest and cream-colored silk cravat.

"Good morning, Papa," she said, bending to kiss her father's cheek.

"Ah, good morning, Kaitie Kathleen, my dear." A hint of Gaelic brogue, evident in his speech from the roll of his R's, was an enduring remnant of his heritage from Scottish ancestry. "What brings you here at this early hour?"

Mr. Trevilian had begun sleeping late in recent months. In his confused state, he thought the hour was 5:30, his usual time to begin the day. He was forever resetting the clocks in the house, saying that they had all been tampered with, that it was some devious Yankee plot to confuse and embarrass the Confederacy.

Amos moved into the room, twisting his hat with trembling hands. He didn't enjoy being a party to deceiving the master.

"Amos, is there a problem in the fields?" Mr. Trevilian questioned, dabbing his mouth with a napkin.

Amos' black eyes darted apprehensively to Kaitland and back to the elderly man.

"Well, speak up, man. I can't solve a problem if I don't know what it is."

"Ah . . . no . . ."

"Amos is helping me today, Papa," Kaitland said, waving a hand casually. "But right now I need your help. We're behind in the ledger entries, and I would like you to join me in the study." She held her breath, not knowing how he would react to the unusual request. It was her hope the suggestion would trigger a memory of what had once been a routine task for him.

After her mother's death, he had spent less and less time with the books, but had still managed to keep the plantation running smoothly. He was always able to find a reason that justified his need to be either in the fields or tending to his prize horses. Kaitland often wondered if the house held too many memories for her father and he needed to escape by spending as much time as he could out of doors.

She had been born late in life to Adeline and Ethan Trevilian. They had given up their hopes of having a family when his beloved wife had become pregnant with Kaitland. Adeline had been thirty-seven years old and Ethan forty-eight. When she died shortly after their daughter's birth, he threw himself into his work. A very prosperous Glen More was the result of overwork and a grief that continued to claim a small piece of him with every breath. Now he was worn, tired, and aged beyond his sixty-nine years.

"Of course. Of course. I was finished with breakfast anyway. These biscuits aren't up to Cook's standards. Perhaps you could have a word with her, Kaitie."

Mr. Trevilian rose a bit more slowly than usual, his forehead creasing as he winced with pain.

Kaitland was instantly at his side, and Amos shuffled over faster than was his habit to lend assistance.

"Papa, are you all right?" she said, troubled eyes fixed on her father's contorted face.

The old man shrugged off their supporting hands and straightened his broad shoulders, adjusting the silk, embroidered vest.

"Of course, I'm fine. It's a little rheumatism. Now wipe that concern from those pretty eyes," he said affectionately, patting the softness of her cheek. "I'm an old man, and a few twinges now and then go with the territory."

His reassuring smile did not fool her. She was sadly aware of his failing health and it tore at her heart to see him this way. She appraised her father with loving eyes. "I know, Papa. Shall we go then?"

"Yes. Yes. By all means. Come along, Amos, and tell me what's been happening with the corn this season."

"Yes, sir. I's comin'. Well, sir. . . ."

Amos began talking about the plantation as it had been before the war. There was no need to bring up the problems they faced. Ethan Trevilian lived and thought in the past, far removed from the effects of the war. Kaitland wanted to keep it that way for as long as possible. Although her efforts on behalf of the plantation were never enough, she was far from beaten. She had her father's Scottish determination and conservatism.

Ethan entered the study and moved toward a large, impressive walnut desk. The room was on the east side of the house and was flooded with the morning sunlight. The smell of leather, tobacco, and beeswax filled the air. It was a man's domain with floor-to-ceiling walnut shelves lined with worn, well-used books. Red leather wing chairs flanked the stone fireplace while two comfortable uphol-stered chairs were arranged near the desk.

"Now, let's see those books that are giving you so much trouble, my dear." Ethan settled himself behind the desk and took up a pen. It all seemed so natural, and Kaitland breathed a sigh of relief.

"They are on the desk, Papa. I'm sure it won't take your experienced eye long to bring them up to date."

She walked behind her father's chair and placed her hands on his broad shoulders, gently kneading the muscles of his neck.

"Would you excuse me, Papa? I want to see Dulcie about the menu for tomorrow."

Her father seemed totally absorbed in his work, and the only acknowledgement he gave was a slight nod, so she quietly slipped from the room.

Kaitland found Christopher in the hall near the back en-trance of the house. As she approached, he studied her, a strange light in his dark eyes. It was his thoughtful ex-pression which puzzled her. He was a paradox, a contra-diction that created an uneasiness in her. One minute he was stern, military in bearing, and the next, thoughtful and caring, a man who protected the enemy. It was becoming increasingly difficult to think of him as an enemy. Until now, she would have found the presence of a Federal of-ficer in the Glen More house completely unacceptable, but somehow this tall stranger had become an exception. Did he think of her as an adversary?

"My father is in the study. You may continue with the search, Lieutenant." She corrected herself as the challenge appeared in his expression. "Christopher."

The corners of his mouth tilted with amusement and he raised a gauntleted hand in mock salute. "Thank you, Kaitland. We shouldn't be much longer. I trust all is well with your father?" He inquired with genuine interest.

"Yes. He is totally unaware of your presence," she said thickly, her long lashes falling softly against her cheeks.

"I'm truly sorry to put you through this but . . ."

She stiffened, regaining her composure. "It's quite all right. I understand. You have a job to do and I must thank you for your consideration." He gave her a neutral look, but she sensed a tangle of emotion in him ready to erupt at any moment. She couldn't help wondering if he was covering his suspicions of her with subterfuge. If this were true, and she fell for his overtures and considerable charm, she ran the risk of capture. Could she trust him? He could be setting a trap.

"You're welcome. If you'll excuse me." He bowed courteously and left, his boots thudding on the bare floor.

The search was completed with little noise or disturbance, and the men were ordered from the house to prepare for departure. Christopher had been as good as his word. None of their property had been disturbed or taken by his men. He had also accepted her word about her father's innocence and avoided contact with him. For that alone, she was most grateful.

Kaitland stood in the foyer watching the troops assemble on the dusty, circular roadway in front of the house. She absently scanned the meticulously kept grounds graced with so many beautiful trees and shrubs.

"I hope we haven't inconvenienced you overmuch,

Kaitland."

The deep resonant voice was unmistakable. It was as though the familiarity had always been a part of her, yet new and exciting. Her heart fluttered as she turned slowly to meet the dark, measuring gaze.

"We'll leave now. I must inform you we will keep Glen More under surveillance. There is the matter of the horse." His voice was suddenly tight, his manner becoming brusque.

"Of course," she replied, her eyes searching his face for some hint of the care she had witnessed there earlier. There was none. Why should she wonder about his moods? He was the enemy, and she owed him nothing.

He had removed his hat and gloves in deference to the rising temperature. He ran his long fingers through the thick, dark brown waves of his neatly trimmed hair, lowering his regard to the toes of his boots. "I'm sorry, Kaitland. There's no excuse for being surly with you. It's certainly not your problem."

A contemplative frown creased his tanned brow, and she was once again drawn into a whirlpool of conflicting emotions he stirred in her. She felt strangely restless and disconcerted, her insides quivering like jelly. "No apologies are necessary, Lieutenant," she said, hoping to sound dispassionate, but certain of her failure.

"Are we back to 'Lieutenant'?" His voice held a chiding note yet it was low and intimate. An easy smile deepened much-used laugh lines.

She attempted to avoid his eyes as she spoke and half turned from him. "Perhaps that would be best. We are worlds apart on probably every issue of life. I understand your orders perfectly. You will receive no resistance to your surveillance from me or this household." Grasping at the shreds of her composure, she turned to meet the enigmatic expression on his face. He took her hand in his and raised it to brush the warmth of a feathery kiss on the sensitive flesh. A small tremor rippled through her.

"If this were another time . . . another place, somehow I feel confident we would find much in common," he murmured, searching her face. His eyes never left hers as he released her.

The soft chimes of the mantel clock broke the silence, and Kaitland's breath caught in her throat under his unrelenting attention. Was he aware that his magnetic virile charm and manner and vibrant timbre of his voice both excited and soothed her?

"I . . . er—" Kaitland closed her eyes and passed a hand over her forehead as if to banish the spell he continued to weave around her. She went on staunchly with great effort, gathering the remnants of placidity.

"Be that as it may, this is not another time or place. We are at war, and I see no point in pursuing further our rela— our acquaintance beyond your professional duty." She furtively held her breath, but was unprepared for his response.

With an agitated movement, Christopher placed the wide-brimmed hat on his head, his features hardening inscrutably as he assumed a military pose, or was it a proud, lonely stance? She couldn't be certain for he abruptly stepped back, brought his fingers to the tip of his hat, saluting her with a curt nod. His eyes bored into hers as he spoke, his voice hard.

"Of course, Miss Trevilian. I'm sorry to have troubled you, but rest assured we will meet again."

The ominous declaration hung heavily between them.

"Is that a threat, Lieutenant?" she said haughtily.

"It's a promise."

He whirled suddenly and crossed the wide porch, the heavy tread of his boots echoing loudly as he descended the stairs, taking two at a time.

"Mount them up, Sergeant."

The explicit, clipped order was barked as he walked with long, determined strides to his waiting horse. Grasping the pommel and swinging into the saddle with ease, he reined the animal so abruptly it nearly sat on its haunches. He hadn't missed the surprise reflected in the faces of his men at the sudden departure. At this moment he simply didn't care. His men knew their place and would never question him.

"Prepare to mount! Mount!"

Leather creaked and strained while the horses grunted and sidestepped under the weight of their riders.

"Right by twos! Column, Ho!"

With the deep voice cadence and familiar rhythm of army commands, the patrol moved forward, the company guidon fluttering with the motion. Dust caught by a sudden breeze swirled up in a powdery cloud from under the cantering hooves of the cavalry horses, covering everything downwind.

Kaitland's eyes never left Christopher's retreating figure, but he rode away without a backward glance. He left as he had ridden into Glen More: straight and tall on his mount, riding easily with the self-assurance of a man born to command.

She had hurt hiim. It was apparent in those magnificent eyes. Why did she care? Regret tightened around her heart as moisture gathered in the wells of her green eyes, blurring the last glimpse of him as he rode through the gates and turned toward the river. She hated this war and what it was doing to the south and her people.

It was more than regret at having offended a fellow human being. There was no excuse for that. Something had happened between them she couldn't explain and she had backed away like a schoolgirl. She wondered if she had convinced herself their political differences was the reason or was she afraid of a developing relationship?

There was so much against them. What if he were to discover her undercover work for the Confederacy? He had made it clear they would meet again. Was it because he suspected her or simply that he meant to see her again? Would he arrest her? She shuddered at the thought as she turned to check on her father.

Christopher had been so kind to protect her father as well as their property, and she had repaid him with an aloof demeanor that was so unnecessary. Had the magnanimous gesture been a ploy to win her confidence, thereby leaving her open to discovery through her carelessness? His concern appeared to be genuine. Had she misjudged him? Surely not. She must, however, not discount the possibility. After all, he was a Federal officer, sworn to uphold the goals and ideals of the government he served. There were so many unanswered questions to ponder.

Kaitland stopped in front of the study door, deep in thought. An anxious sigh escaped her trembling lips. If only she had someone in whom she could confide, but there was no one. She was alone with an aging father who knew little of the circumstances that surrounded them. The up-keep of their huge plantation required more hours than there were in a day with their more than one hundred slaves waiting for direction. If that weren't enough, she had set a course for herself that was, in some ways, more dangerous than going into battle.

Feeling sorry for herself would accomplish nothing. She couldn't give up in the face of this most recent development. It simply meant she would have to be more careful. Raising her chin and forcing a smile, Kaitland opened the study door.

"Papa, how are you coming with the ledgers?"

four

"Kaitland, I can't understand how you manage this great plantation all by yourself. Why if my mama and papa weren't with me, I don't know what I'd do."

Lucinda Monroe's whining voice droned on while she daintily sipped tea from Glen More's best imported china. She was a tall young woman, bone thin, but possessing a rather pretty face. Her most endearing quality was an abundance of beautiful pale-blond wavy hair which she arranged to her best advantage. Kaitland tried to envision the immaculately dressed Lucinda in trousers, embarking upon a night ride alone to carry messages to the Confederate command. She smothered a giggle as the humor of such a happening flitted through her mind.

"I manage quite well, Lucinda. I'm really not alone. My father—"

"Now, Kaitland, don't try to be so brave. We've known each other too long for pretense. Your father's condition is no secret among our neighbors."

Kaitland stiffened, and she felt an angry flush heightening the natural color of her face. Why did people find it necessary to entertain themselves with idle gossip about the misfortune of others?

Lucinda had been a friend of Kaitland's since they were children. Though they were not as close as Lucinda would like to believe, Kaitland enjoyed her company. At least she was another female her own age. She suspected the reason for her visit was to learn all she could about the Union patrol. News traveled fast, and Lucinda usually intercepted every tidbit spreading through a three-county area.

"Really, Lucinda, must you encourage such talk? My father simply doesn't feel well. He suffers from chronic rheumatism and has relinquished some responsibilities of management to me." To stave off Lucinda's natural over-active curiosity was an exercise in bantering chatter. The young woman eyed Kaitland over the rim of her cup, a knowing look in her expression.

"As you wish, my dear, but I've heard—"

"Please try one of Suzie's pastries. They really are quite good, considering we must use molasses for a sweetening agent these days." Anxious to change the subject, Kaitland blurted the words unnaturally, her hand unsteady as she passed the lead crystal dish to her friend.

"Thank you." The young woman placed a delicious-looking cream puff on her plate, scarcely pausing for breath or acknowledging a shift in their conversation.

"Now you must tell me about the Yankee Army that invaded Glen More."

The inquisitive visitor leaned forward, dropping her voice conspiratorially. Her eyes were wide with interest as she pulled a lacy square of Cambric from the cuff of her blouse. She raised the handkerchief to her mouth, convinced that what she was about to hear would be scandalous.

Ah, there it is. The true reason for Lucinda's visit surfaced, but Kaitland was determined to downplay the incident. It was important to draw as little attention to herself as possible.

"In the first place, Lucinda, it was only a patrol, not an entire army, and they didn't invade Glen More. They were simply looking for an informant and conducted an orderly search, then left. That's all there was to it."

"Spy!" Lucinda's mouth was as round as her eyes. "Oh, Kaitland, weren't you frightened beyond words? Why, I'm certain I would suffer an attack of the vapors if Yankees ever searched our house. Papa would have no compunction about opening fire if Yankee soldiers dared to ride up to our house," she said, waving a small fan rapidly just under her slender chin.

Kaitland could imagine the portly Mr. Monroe blustering through the main house of Boxwood Plantation to take a stand on the threshold of his gallery.

"No, I was not frightened. The lieutenant was most courteous." Christopher Donovan had occupied her thoughts more than she cared to admit since his angry departure three days ago.

"You always were the daring one, even when we were children. You had a penchant for hiding from me in the woods and riding those disgusting horses." Lucinda wrinkled her nose, then gave a long-suffering sigh. "Nothing ever frightened you."

"Well, I really must go. Thank you for tea and do come for a visit soon, Kaitland. You stay to yourself too much. Perhaps we can have a small dinner party soon. It would take our minds off this dreadful war, you know." She pulled on dainty white lace gloves while making her way to the door. Her felicitous mood set Kaitland's teeth on edge, but she could not help smiling at the abrupt decision to leave.

Dear Lucinda could not wait to spread what she had learned about the patrol. An incurable gossip, the fluttery young woman failed to realize she had not discovered anything of real consequence. Kaitland was certain the truth would become an insignificant fragment among a series of distortions and pure fiction in her friend's dramatization of the event.

"A party sounds delightful. I'll be in touch soon."

"Good-bye, Kaitland," she cooed, leaning forward, kissing the air near Kaitland's cheek, bustling away in a flurry of taffeta petticoats and hooped skirts.

Walking slowly back to the parlor, Kaitland sat on the red velvet settee and picked up her teacup. Why did a certain handsome lieutenant occupy so much of her thinking? She was a little uncomfortable exploring that question too deeply. The impact of his visit had dominated and interfered with her work for three days, and no man had ever held her attention that long before.

"Miz Kaitland."

Amos' voice startled her back to the present. "Oh, yes, Amos, what is it?"

"Well, I is wonderin' if you is goin' t' ride out t' da fields t'day."

"No, Amos. It can wait until tomorrow. Saddle Stardust for me, please. I'd like to take a ride to the brook and sit for a while," she said, sighing absently. She needed a few hours to herself. The demands of running the plantation combined with the tension from her secret activities were draining her.

"Yes, 'um. I saddle her for you. I sure am glad dem Yankees didn't take dat hoss of your papa's since he means so much t' him."

"Amos, did you hear the men talking while they were here? I mean . . . did you overhear any of their plans?" She should have asked him sooner, but she didn't seem to do anything right lately.

"No, 'um. Jist men talk mostly. Dat lieutenant watched 'um real close. I don't think he wants t' be here. I heard him say he wished he was with dat Gen'ral McClellan when he started up da York River."

"What!" Kaitland jumped up and whirled to face the old man. "Why didn't you tell me this, Amos?"

"Well, it didn't strike me as real impor'ant. I mean . . . I—"

"I'm sorry, Amos. It's just that everything is important with a war at our doorstep."

"But, Miz Kaitland, he say da York River. We lives on da James. How's dat—"

"Amos, if McClellan chooses to steam up the York River, it will place Federal troops on the peninsula, and if successful, they could march right past us to Richmond."

"Lausy, Mis Kaitland, you mean dem Yankees goin' t' tromp right through Glen More?" he said, eyes wide with fear.

"That's exactly what I mean."

"Lausy, lausy, what we gonna do? Dat would upset da mas'r somethin' awful!" the old Negro said, turning his big head from side to side. "Yes, sir, jist awful."

She took his roughened hand in hers. "Bless you, Amos. You're always thinking of Papa. Don't worry, I'll try to get a message through to command in Richmond."

"Miz Kaitland, you ain't thinkin' o' goin' all da way t'

Richmond alone, is you?"

"No, you're going with me. We'll go tomorrow. It's too late to make the journey today. Have the buggy ready at daybreak. I must attempt to see General Johnston. If anyone asks, just say I'm going shopping."

"Yes, 'um. I be ready. Ain't nothin' gonna happen t' you on dis ride," he said assuringly, a broad grin changing his concerned features to those of satisfaction.

"Thanks, old friend. I'm sure I could never be safer. Now, suppose you get Stardust for me," she said smiling.

"Yes, 'um, I do dat right now. Yes, um, right now."

The mare danced and sidled, eager to be off. She had been neglected lately with Kaitland preferring Prince for her secret missions. The large mare was easily guided from the stable as they turned southeast.

There was a small brook tripping through a lush meadow at the lower end of their property. It was her favorite place in all the world, and she frequented the seclusion of the huge, sheltering elms near the brook as often as possible.

The somnolent early April afternoon sun filtered through the thickly wooded area as she made her way through blooming dogwood to the quiet haven. It was warm for April, urging Mother Nature into an early display of spring colors, and new life.

Passing an old split rail fence, she approached the meadow and heard the inviting, tranquil sound of running water rushing over and around the rocks. She dismounted and led Stardust to a tall stand of grass in a copse of trees. After tying her to a small oak, she walked to the stream and stood gazing at the meadow on the other side. It was encircled by budding trees. Sunlight dappled the idyllic scene, creating a sense of inner peace far removed from the misery of war and the stress of everyday life.

Kaitland slipped the loop that caught up the skirt of her riding habit over her wrist and sat down, resting against the rough bark of a tree by the water's edge. She loosened the top two buttons of her jacket to cool her flushed skin. As she slowly removed her gloves she could feel the tension flowing from her body.

Fatigue had become her close companion lately, but sleep would come only after hours of tossing and turning far into the night, and she would waken before dawn. So many new problems and complications had risen, especially since the visit of the Union patrol. She had not been called upon for further service to the Confederacy since then, and that was just as well. If she were being watched, it would be difficult to slip away unnoticed. But tomorrow shouldn't pose a problem. Frequent trips to Richmond were not unusual.

Kaitland watched the flickering rays of the sun casting its beams through the green bows overhead. She removed her jockey hat, and placed it on the moss-covered ground beside her. The earthy smells and sounds of the woods enveloped her, filling her senses. As she relaxed, letting her mind float free, her eyelids became heavy and slowly she drifted into a peaceful, exhausted slumber.

She had no idea how long she had slept, but consciousness gradually returned, prompted by aching muscles from the awkward position, or had she heard an unfamiliar sound? Her eyes fluttered open, weighted from sleep as the image of a tall figure came into focus. The sun made a crescent around its head, creating a dreamy, fuzzy picture.

He was so tall.

"Christopher," she whispered, smiling lazily.

"Christopher!" Kaitland jumped up, nearly losing her balance, wincing from the sudden demands on sore muscles.

"Hey, take it easy. I didn't mean to startle you." He chuckled as he grasped her shoulders to steady her. "You were sleeping so peacefully I didn't want to disturb you."

"How long have you been here?" she asked breathlessly, staring at him in disbelief.

"Oh, about half an hour."

"You've been watching me for thirty minutes?" She pulled away from him and took a step backward. "Of all the—"

"Now don't get your dander up. I didn't have the heart to waken you. When I saw you last, it appeared to me you could use some sleep."

The sudden anger Kaitland felt ebbed, and she tensed, becoming alert to the possible implications of a seemingly innocuous statement. He was more perceptive than she had imagined. He had been aware of her loss of sleep through an astute appraisal three days ago. If she were a consummate actress, playing innocent might come more easily, but to be constantly on her guard was unnerving.

"Yes . . . well, I haven't slept well recently. The burden of so many decisions to make without my father's input has been . . . difficult."

She avoided his eyes, turning toward her horse, who was still tied, contentedly munching on the abundant grass.

"Of course," he said, suddenly realizing she intended to leave, and he couldn't let that happen, not now.

"Kaitland, please stay for a while and talk. Surely you

don't have to hurry off just yet."

Christopher moved forward and stood behind her, his elongated shadow falling over her like a thundercloud. She could feel his closeness, the heat radiating from his body drawing her to him. When she turned, her eyes fell on the yoked uniform blouse with the Federal Army insignia on the brass buttons. Why hadn't she thought to ask him his reason for being here? What was he doing on her property again? Somehow she was certain the answer would not be what she cared to hear, even if he were being truthful.

"No, I suppose it isn't imperative that I leave now." It was so easy to unwittingly tumble into the dark depths of his eyes, feeling the tension rising to feverish excitement.

"Why are you here, Christopher?" she said, her mind not really on the question or the answer.

"Oh, that isn't important. Just army matters. I was taking a shortcut. Come and sit for a while." He took her hand and led her back to the brook's edge where they sat down on the soft green moss covering the bank.

The evasiveness of his answer bothered her, but what did she expect? He wouldn't reveal his reason for being on her land. She had made it clear she would not interfere with his work. The information she had received from Amos was making her even more suspicious. If General McClellan was on the brink of an invasion, and that seemed to be the case, then why was Christopher still in the area, unless he remained under orders to find the informant. It was so difficult to think about the war with this magnificent man so close to her. *Another time. Another place.* Those had been his exact words. She wondered if he still felt the same way.

"I like the sound." Christopher broke the silence.

"What!" She turned to stare at him. He was so handsome sitting there, his leg drawn up with one arm casually resting on the bent knee.

"You used my name again instead of lieutenant. I like the sound when you say it. Your accent gives a certain air to an otherwise ordinary name."

"Are you poking fun at my accent?" she snapped defensively.

"Of course not. I only meant . . . is that what you think?"

"No. I know what you meant. I'm sorry for lashing out at you. I don't know why I do that."

Christopher laughed and stretched out on the ground, his hands clasped behind his head. "Apology accepted. There's a lot of fire under that cool, prim demeanor you project, Miss Trevilian."

She smiled to herself. Those were almost the same words her father had used to describe her many times, usually when he was upset with her. "I try so hard to overcome these sudden bursts of anger."

Christopher raised himself on one elbow, capturing her attention before she could finish her thought. "Don't ever change, Kaitland, not ever." His words were solemn, almost desperate. "You're the only woman I have ever met with such determination and innate ability to survive. I've observed the vast area you manage, and you accomplish more than a lot of men I know."

He smiled. His tone became light and teasing as he resumed his previous position. "Anyway, I like women with spirit. They make life exciting."

"Oh? I'm sure you've known many women, but of

course, that's really none of my concern," she said haughtily, her eyes sparkling with silent challenge.

"Shall I tell you about them?" he said mockingly, still teasing, raising up again on one elbow to watch her.

"Certainly not!" She angled her chin out to feign an attitude of insult, but when she looked back at him and saw the mischievous sparkle in his eyes, they both laughed.

The playful exchange eased the tension, making possible a relaxed, natural conversation. Kaitland wanted that very much. She found herself enjoying his company more than any man she had ever met, being drawn irresistibly to him. She wondered if he felt the same way or were his motives something else? His admiration for her was evident, but that did not mean he wouldn't try to trick her into saying something incriminating.

"Now this is what I call a pleasant afternoon. I've looked forward to seeing you again, Kaitland." He studied her in the gathering silence.

She thought for a moment. "Have you? Frankly, I never expected to see you again. You were quite angry when you left." Plucking at a blade of grass, she recalled his breakneck departure three days ago.

"That was frustration. I had finally met a woman unlike any I'd met before, and this blasted war puts us on opposite sides," he said defeatedly, draping one arm over his eyes.

"How do you feel about the war? Do you have the slightest understanding of our position?"

She was aware her question could very well grow into a heated argument as she had observed many times in recent years. She thought of men pounding tables, striking heroic arrogant poses, adamant in their opinionated ravings. Her desire to know how he felt overruled the possibility. His thoughts had become important to her. Lord forbid that anyone should find them there together. She would have a lot of explaining to do, but it didn't seem to matter.

A long pause followed. Christopher stirred and crossed his long legs at the ankles, the heavy leather boots squeaking with the friction.

"Yes, I can understand. I think economics has dictated man's actions for centuries, and this war is no exception."

"How is that?" Her inquiry was rooted in genuine interest as she shifted to a more comfortable position.

"The South has acquired great wealth and aristocratic position with the use of the slave system. I think this fact strikes fear among many in the North. While most Southerners will admit the use of slaves is morally wrong, they find it necessary for the land to be productive. Elimination of the South's sizable investment would be economic suicide. I believe the system would be abandoned if another form of labor could be found."

Kaitland listened intently to his calm analysis of the causes of this war. She watched the play of emotions on his face, for his eyes were closed.

"You know, the practice is still legal in several northern states including the District of Columbia?" The irony in his chuckle was unmistakable. "It's a bit like the pot calling the kettle black. I'm afraid raising the slavery issue as a major cause of this war is so much hypocritical gumbeating. The war is the result of sectional rivalry and political ambition. I think the war would have eventually taken place even if there had never been a Negro in America.

Slavery has simply served as a catalyst for the prejudices and sympathies of the people to come into focus."

Christopher moved up several notches on her scale of respect with that last statement. Too many people had laid the entire cause of the war at the doorstep of slavery. He was certainly better informed than she expected.

"It comes as no surprise that a very small number of slave masters are fighting for the Confederacy. The sad fact remains that the South has little knowledge of war. You see, the South's economy is primarily based on agriculture, and your industry has been hastily assembled. I'm afraid your people will be asked to make tremendous sacrifices if the war continues for a long period of time. Of course, there are many things in your favor," he said with a smile. "Your admirable enthusiasm and the fervor with which you take a stand isn't to be taken lightly. The South's dedication is to be admired, even by a Yankee."

"What about states' rights?" she said without taking note of his attempt to inject humor into the seriousness of the conversation.

He opened one eye and looked at her, smiling lazily. "You certainly are inquisitive," he said, his voice threaded with satisfied amusement.

Kaitland lowered her lashes, concealing the excitement that would certainly be revealed in her eyes. She knew so little about this handsome northerner, but his company did strange things to her. She could listen to him for hours. He talked to her as an equal, something few men were inclined to do.

"Very well, lovely lady. Let's see, states' rights," he said with a sigh and closed his eyes again. "I know many secessionists believe that national government is a league of sovereign states, thereby giving any state the legal right to withdraw from the Union. States' rights is certainly an important factor and I believe one of the major causes of this madness."

Silence followed as Kaitland thought about his words. "Christopher, you're saying that the South's position is proper, but you must win. The South is politically divided in many quarters, I'll admit, but we waited to secede until a sectional president was nominated and elected by a sectional convention and vote. The shocking thing is that your president came to office by a vote of a minority of the people. We tried union despite unequal tariff laws. How could anyone deny the systematic and persistent attempt to deprive the southern states of equality in the Union? Our motivation was and remains freedom. We just want to be assured that constitutional government is accomplished. I can't believe we could lose the war. How can you have a divided allegiance?" Her voice was weighted with the frustration and confusion she felt.

Frowning, he sat up and faced her, his relaxed features of a moment ago became clouded and serious. "I do not have a divided allegiance, Kaitland. That's just how I view the war. My allegiance lies with the Union. It doesn't mean I approve of war. I hate it!" he said vehemently. "It is nothing but unnecessary killing, destruction, and breaking the backs of proud people!

"I wish there were a way to save the South, but it's gone too far. They are doing well now, but their efforts will ultimately fail. War will not accomplish your goals."

He released a slow shaky breath and stood up, turning

his back to her. It was plain to see his heart wasn't in his work where the war was concerned. She was curious to know if the military was his chosen career. If he felt so strongly, how could he serve with the Union? It was impossible to think of the South's defeat.

"We seem to be saying the same things, but differing on methods and results," she admitted in a small voice.

"So it would appear," he said flatly.

"Do you plan to stay in the army after this is all over?"

He turned to face her, his towering frame casting its shadow over her. The lines of his face softened, and his maleness overpowered her. She fought to maintain a thread of thought. He stretched languidly, apparently satisfied with the shift in their conversation.

"No. At one time I thought the army was what I wanted. My father is in shipping in New York. He wanted me to join him in the business, but I was a bit rebellious then and entered West Point instead. Now at thirty-four, I want out of this uniform to go home and help my father. He's getting along in years and needs me."

Christopher lowered himself to one knee, taking her hands in his warm grasp. "I've talked too much. Now, tell me about yourself."

He dropped down beside her, his closeness was so vital and strong. Their budding relationship seemed impossible. Everything was against them . . . except how she felt now.

"What do you want to know?" she asked brightly, his interest sending a surge of anticipation through her.

"Tell me about Glen More. Where did the name come from?"

"It's named for a valley in Scotland where my grandparents came from. When they came to this country, they started with five hundred acres. As the years passed, more and more land was acquired until it reached its present size of about four thousand acres."

"It's a big job for one so small," he said, his eyes holding her captive. "How do you manage this big place virtually alone?"

"I'm afraid I don't manage all that well. So much is left undone, and I'm short of workers. The only options left are to reduce some of the crops or to sell the stock. If the war continues much longer . . ." She studied her hands and fell silent for a few moments.

"My father has supported the Confederacy financially since its conception. That has drained much of our reserves necessary to maintain peak production. Of course, I depend a great deal on my faith."

Christopher's questioning silence and intensity of his expression sent a shiver down her spine. He suddenly pulled away, and she felt an invisible barrier springing up between them. What had she said to cause this sudden shift in his mood?

"Are you telling me God has been running this plantation?" His words were tinged with incredulity and, she thought, a hint of sarcasm.

"Of course not. I meant He supplies me with the necessary strength and wisdom to continue despite the odds." A horrible thought struck her with tremendous force. "Don't you believe in God, Christopher?" She held her breath waiting for his answer.

"Oh, I believe in a Supreme Being, but I can't say He has ever given me much help," he said casually, yet almost sardonically, gesturing with his hand.

"Have you ever asked for His help?" she said, feeling relieved. At least he didn't deny the existence of God.

"I suppose I did as a child at the urging of my mother. She was a devout Christian. She died when I was twelve. I try to believe she's in a better world, but I don't know," he said doubtfully, anger and resentment creeping into his voice.

The softening of his tone when he mentioned his mother was almost reverent. Kaitland bit her lip, frowning thoughtfully. "She is, Christopher. You must believe that. If she were a Christian, she would want you to know that."

"I suppose," he finally said with skepticism. He walked to the edge of the water, picked up some small pebbles, and sent them skittering across the stream.

"Kaitland, if you're a Christian, how can you justify holding human beings in bondage and supporting a war that has the preservation of that system as one of its objectives?"

"Our workers are well cared for. Most of them are very faithful and enjoy their way of life," she said pleadingly, her hands outstretched. She was standing now, moving to face him. "I know the situation isn't ideal on all plantations. Some workers are exploited and abused, but it isn't like that at Glen More."

"They are still slaves, are they not?" he said in hard tones, his voice rising. "You can't even say the word. You call them workers, yet they are not freemen. They are slaves, Kaitland."

The veracity of his statement stung, and she winced from the accusation. "Christopher, you're twisting—"

"Yes or no."

She realized how his attitude had drastically changed when she had mentioned her faith. Somehow talking about God triggered an anger in him over which he seemed to have little control.

"Yes," she whispered, lowering her eyes to the soft grass underfoot, a catch in her throat. He was searching for answers to justify his point of view.

"There seems to be a contradiction somewhere, wouldn't you say?" His statement didn't ring with triumph as she had expected.

"I never looked at it quite like that." She turned away from him, unwilling to reveal the wave of emotion she was certain he could read in her face.

He had raised an issue that stirred a conflict within her a great deal lately. In her heart of hearts she knew slavery was wrong. Despite this conflict, the South could not lose the war. It would be destroyed or crippled for generations to come.

The stern lines of his face softened as he exhaled slowly. "I'm sorry, Kaitland. I had no right to question your motives. It was not my intention to create a problem for you. It's just that I feel so strongly about slavery."

The genuine regret in his voice touched her. He moved and stood close behind her placing his hands on her upper arms.

"You needn't apologize. Your point is well taken."

They stood there among the trees for many minutes, his chin resting on the top of her head. The war seemed remote and unimportant at that moment. Her entire world was in a turmoil, but the breathless calm around them was all that she yearned for now. His touch was warm, making her feel safe and secure for the first time in over a year.

Christopher's strong hands began massaging her arms, then he turned her around to face him. He cupped her cheek with one hand and trailed a finger down the delicate curve of her chin.

"I want to see you again. I don't know how or when with this craziness all around us, but we can't leave it this way." His dark eyes drew her into their warmth, spinning a web around them, insulating them from the world.

"I don't think it would be a good idea. We can't . . . I mean—" She lost her thought as he lowered his head, blocking out the sun. Her heart raced frantically as his arms pulled her closer. Her mind rebelled, but emotions and instincts overruled logic as an uncontrollable heat flooded through her, washing away the last threads of restraint.

He groaned as his lips found hers. She leaned into the hardness of his muscled body. His hand slid up to caress her neck. A rapturous moan slipped from her throat in response to his touch. She had never experienced anything like this before. His kiss commanded, implored and coaxed her into a vortex from which there was no return.

"Kaitland," he whispered huskily against her ear, then her lips.

"Oh, this is all wrong," she murmured weakly. "We can't—"

"Don't say that. Nothing could be so right."

His arms tightened around her, and he held her with a desperation that frightened yet lured and captivated her. Torn between propriety and a consuming desire so new to her, she moved out of his arms with great effort because she wanted desperately to stay.

"I must go. It's getting late, and my father will be asking for me." Her words were disjointed and sounded strange to her. She made an effort to straighten her hair, smoothing loosened strands back into place. With trembling hands she pinned the small plumed hat to her hair.

"Kaitland."

The way he said her name sounded so helpless, pleading.

"Meet me here again. I'll send a message when I can arrange it. Please say yes."

She couldn't resist the entreaty in his voice and especially his eyes. She was nodding as she took the reins and prepared to mount. "All right, I'll try."

Christopher moved with lithe, muscular control to help her mount, but she was already in the saddle, riding away in a flurry. She soon questioned the prudence of her promise to him. The more involved she became, the more dangerous her position. Tomorrow she was to see General Johnston about what may very well be the largest campaign of the war, and she was becoming involved with a Federal officer. She no longer cared about gaining information from him. He was too clever for that anyway. Her only motive for seeing him again was purely personal. She hoped she did not live to regret the decision.

The conflict tearing her apart at this moment was staggering. How would she ever extricate herself from this mess? Taking the information to General Johnston could mean Christopher would be caught up in a battle that— she must not dwell on that now. The encounter would take place no matter what she did. If she did not deliver the message, Richmond could fall and the war would be over. She was torn between a commitment to the South and a man who had come to mean a great deal to her.

☙

Christopher watched Kaitland until she disappeared in the trees. The afternoon sun filtered through the branches, the shadows further obscuring her retreating figure. His emotions were becoming entangled with this beautiful, desirable woman, and he knew his increasing attraction to her could ultimately affect his investigation. If she were the spy he sought, she was more of a woman than anyone realized. Unfortunately, he did believe she was the Confederate informant. God help him if he found enough evidence to arrest her.

five

The morning air was cold and heavy, made drearier by thick gray clouds skudding overhead with rain threatening at any moment. The buggy moved swiftly along Osborne Turnpike, three miles from Richmond. Amos was quieter than usual as he managed with ease the large bay which pulled their small conveyance. The mare was harness shy and a bit skittish because of infrequent use in recent months. Kaitland had little need for a buggy in the work she did for the Confederacy.

A chilling drizzle began to fall as they approached the intersection of Osborne Turnpike and River Road. The oiled, canvas top protected them for a while, but gusts of wind sent stinging icy raindrops into their faces.

Kaitland snuggled into the heavy lap robe, pulling it closer in an effort to stay warm. She had not given much thought to proper attire that morning. Fortunately, Dulcie had laid out a warm hooded cloak, anticipating the penetrating chill in the air. An added luxury was her chincilla muff that she took at the last minute.

From her vantage point riding along the banks of the James River, she had a sweeping view of the skyline and Tredegar Iron works. It was from this industry that the lifeline of the war flowed into the Richmond Armory and other plants. Richmond had become the political, military, and manufacturing center of the South, the symbol of secession to the North. What better target for a massive invasion than the very heartbeat of the Confederate states?

The consensus of opinion was that Richmond's demise would mean the fall of the Confederacy. The city's population had doubled as people came flocking in search of jobs. The government departments, the arms and uniform manufacturing plants were all located here. It seemed the policy of the Confederacy had been to concentrate the production of supplies at the Capitol.

"We is 'most there, Mis Kaitlan'," Amos said reassuringly. "Git up, hoss. Move dem feet." The old man snapped the leather reins on the horse's rump, urging the animal into a faster trot.

"I'm all right, Amos. My business shouldn't take long, and we can hurry back to Glen More before the road becomes too slippery for travel. This could turn into a steady downpour," she said above the persistent tattoo of rain pelting the buggy. She looked warily at the ominous clouds, the boiling elements matching her state of mind. It was a miserable day, made worse by her obsessive memory of the chance meeting with Christopher yesterday.

Sleep had eluded her until nearly dawn. After tossing for hours, she had finally fallen into a fitful, restless slumber only to awaken feeling weary of body and spirit. Christopher's eyes had haunted her at night as well as during the hours of consciousness. He was not a man to be forgotten. Her growing attraction to him both thrilled and frightened her. It was incredible that after only two meetings she could feel so strongly drawn to him. It defied explanation. She could still feel the warmth of his touch, the slight tremor of his lips touching hers.

Their relationship was completely unrealistic and that troubled her. The standards for proper conduct set by society and her upbringing could not stop the overwhelming rush of complex emotions Christopher's presence stirred in her. He brought life to a part of her she never knew existed. Surely, there could not be anything wrong with a strong, genuine attraction between two adults. In her heart she felt no remorse, only a longing that she was at a loss to explain. How could she reconcile reason with the joy coursing through her?

Who was she kidding? Deluding herself into believing there could ever be anything between them was nothing short of insanity. They were enemies, and nothing could change that. Yet how could she deny the way he made her feel?

The buggy swerved, jolting her back to the present from her reverie. She had nearly canceled this trip after visiting her father that morning. He hadn't looked well at all. He had seemed more confused than usual. His skin had turned ashen gray, his lips slightly blue. It was difficult to leave, but Dulcie had assured her she would keep a constant vigil.

Kaitland knew time was of the essence in reaching General Johnston, and if her father had been well he would have been the first to encourage haste.

"Miz Kaitlan', is you feelin' aw right? You is mighty quiet." Amos' furrowed brow and wide eyes reflected his concern.

"What? Oh, yes, Amos. I was just thinking about Papa. He didn't look well this morning. I didn't want to leave him," she answered with a deep sigh.

"Now don't you go worrin' 'bout your papa. My Dulcie

gonne take real fine care o' da mas'r."

"Amos, you are always so reassuring. I know he couldn't be in better hands."

"Yes, 'um, dat's a fact," Amos said with unmistakable pride.

The remainder of the journey was completed in silence. The weather settled down to a steady, gusting rain. Amos stopped the buggy in front of General Johnston's headquarters, a large brick building near the White House of the Confederacy. They had been directed there after a few inquiries.

In the distance, Kaitland could see Thomas Jefferson's stately capitol building on Shockoe Hill. As long as the Stars and Bars were fluttering in the breeze, the people felt secure that the Confederate States of America was a going concern.

"Yes, ma'am, may I help you?" asked the bearded captain seated behind a desk.

Kaitland looked around at the spacious foyer with its beautiful marbled walls and floors. She could see into an adjacent room to her right where a roaring fire was blazing in a mammoth fireplace, the hearth and mantel the same shiny gray marble.

"Yes, thank you, Captain. I'm Kaitland Trevilian from Glen More Plantation on the James. I have an urgent message for General Johnston."

"Well, I'm not sure that ..." he said uncertainly, toying with a pen.

"Please, Captain, this is of the utmost importance."

"Have a seat, Miss Trevilian. I'll see what can be arranged." He rose and walked the length of the elegant hall and knocked on a door.

Kaitland sat down, grateful for an opportunity to warm herself before seeing the general. It wouldn't do for her teeth to be chattering at a time like this.

Moments later the young soldier emerged from the room. "Miss Trevilian, the general will see you now."

The officer stood at attention as Kaitland entered, then quietly closed the door.

General Johnston rose and extended his hand over a cluttered oak desk. "Miss Trevilian, I believe. I'm General Johnston."

The man's kindly eyes and gentle manner put her at ease immediately. He was in full uniform except for the sword, which lay on his desk to one side. Hanging on the wall behind his chair were the Confederate and the Virginia State flags, the colors bold and stirring. Pride swelled in her chest as she placed her hand in the General's firm grasp.

"Thank you for seeing me so promptly, sir."

"Won't you be seated and tell me this important news," he inquired, gesturing toward a chair in front of his desk. The general took his seat after she had arranged her skirt and sat down. He paused for a moment and slid a crooked index finger over a neatly trimmed mustache, then smoothed his small goatee.

"May I order some refreshments while we speak?" he said graciously.

"No thank you, sir. I haven't much time, so I'll get to the point. Earlier this week our plantation was searched by a Union patrol. They were looking for a spy—"

"A spy! Trevilian. Trevilian," he mumbled to himself, as if searching his memory for a connection between the two.

"Ah, yes, Trevilian." A triumphant gleam appeared in his steel-gray eyes as he raised his bushy brows. "Now I remember. Your name has been mentioned in connection with . . . shall we say some rather secret activities?" A knowing smile further creased the lines in his aging face.

"Forgive me for interrupting, my dear, but I'm pleased to meet you. Your reputation precedes you, and your assistance is greatly appreciated by the Confederacy."

"Thank you, General. You're very kind. I haven't had the opportunity to do a great deal, but I'm only too happy to pass on anything of importance."

"At great risk to yourself, it seems. I am well aware of the dangers our spies of the Confederacy face. Many have distinguished themselves time and again. Their bravery has often made the difference between defeat and victory in numerous battles. The patrol found nothing, I assume, since you are here." He grinned amiably.

"Only my horse, but there was no way to prove it was I who had been riding him. Their suspicions, however, have been aroused, and I must be very careful. I'm certain my activities are being watched."

"By all means, my dear. You must be extremely careful. The Confederacy values highly its heroic women. Now, you must be here concerning another matter." Folding his hands on top of the desk, the general leaned forward with interest.

"During the search, a trusted servant overheard the lieutenant in charge state he would rather be with McClellan when he starts up the York River. I felt this was important since a massive invasion is apparently imminent and the route the Federals take is vital to our defense."

The information she revealed so easily did not give her the personal satisfaction she had expected. Somehow she felt she had betrayed Christopher. How was this possible? She was a Virginian, a loyal Southerner, and a staunch supporter of the Confederacy. She believed in what they were doing; yet, an overwhelming sense of loss came over her. Christopher had nearly convinced her the South would inevitably lose the war. Was this all for naught?

"Indeed, it is very important. This confirms our intelligence reports. The Confederacy is indebted to you. From all information, this may well be the largest amphibious operation ever attempted in the Western world."

"Miss Trevilian," he said hesitantly, smoothing his goatee. "Could you find a Confederate unit near your home?" He seemed to be studying her face, perhaps searching for any sign of fear or indecision. "Why, yes, General. I know the approximate locations of our soldiers on the James near us." Her interest heightened. She could feel her heart race with anticipation.

"I detect an eagerness in you, Miss Trevilian, that encourages me to take a drastic step. Would you be willing to carry a message to a patrol near your plantation? General A.P. Hill is in the field on the peninsula gathering information as to the strength and capabilities of enemy forces. I must dispatch a message to him. A courier such as yourself might be the most judicious choice." She was about to respond when the general raised his hand to stop her.

"Before you answer, I must warn you that carrying a written message is far more dangerous than the verbal information you have just given me. Perhaps you need time to think about it. I would certainly understand."

"No. That won't be necessary. I'm committed to the cause, and I cannot pick and choose the manner in which I do my part. I would be honored to carry the dispatch, and I will do my very best to see that it is delivered."

A week ago she would have been ecstatic with an assignment such as this. It was indeed an honor to be entrusted with the general's confidence. Where was the elation? Where was her spirit? *Christopher, what have you done to me,* she thought, her heartbeat fluctuating.

"Good! I'll just be a moment. I'm certain you wish to return home before this weather makes traveling impossible," he said, having already taken up a pen.

Kaitland sat quietly while General Johnston wrote hurriedly and sealed the official note.

"There," he said with satisfaction, handing the missive to her. "If you determine at anytime that this letter may be intercepted or your mission may be discovered, destroy this paper without delay. Richmond must be saved at all costs."

"I understand. Thank you for seeing me and entrusting this to my care." She folded the sealed paper and carefully placed it in her small, black, velvet handbag. The seriousness of this responsibility was evident in his penetrating eyes, and a slight tremor of fear charged through her.

"Take care, child. These are perilous times in which we live."

Kaitland noticed for the first time the gaunt fatigue lines on the older man's face. The tremendous weight of the burden he carried on his shoulders was reflected in the weary stance of his body.

"I will, General. Good-bye."

The journey back to Glen More was arduous and trying. Cold rain mixed with sleet fell steadily, turning the road into a slippery, treacherous quagmire of oozing, sucking mud. If it had not been for Amos' skill in handling the rig, they would have become bogged down several times. When they finally reached the main house, their clothes were soaked through to the skin. Kaitland was so tired and hungry she could barely put one foot in front of the other. All she wanted was a hot bath and the warmth of her bed. She had tried to eat the lunch Dulcie had prepared, but it stuck in her throat. Conflicting thoughts and emotions tormented her troubled mind, refusing logical or sensible reasoning.

Dulcie met her at the front door, swinging it wide to embrace her mistress against an ample bosom. Kaitland was so tired, she missed the old woman's agitated state and her tearstained plump cheeks.

Suddenly, Kaitland felt uneasy. A sense of forboding washed over her. Something was wrong. Fear surged through her, alerting her fatigued mind.

"Dulcie, what is it? What's happened?"

"Oh, Miz Kaitland." Before she could utter another word, she broke into great heaving sobs.

Kaitland stood unmoving for a few moments, stunned by the servant's emotional outburst. Then Amos rushed through the door breathing heavily.

"What you bawlin' 'bout, Dulcie?" He grabbed her by the shoulders and gave her a sound shake. "Come on. Git holt o' yourself, woman. I was 'most to da stable, and I could hear you wailin' way down da road."

"Oh, Amos, it's da mas'r." Her words were disjointed and punctuated with sobs.

Kaitland felt her chilled body suddenly grow numb. Her knees threatened to buckle. Blood pounded in her ears with deafening force, and her heart felt as though it might burst from the pressure.

"What about Papa?" she asked softly, frozen to the floor, a puddle of water forming around her feet, dripping from her rainsoaked clothes. Violent chills began to wrack her body, but she tried not to notice.

Dulcie turned to face her, tears streaming from her painridden eyes. "Oh, chil', I so sorry t' tell you dis, but your Papa, he done went t' da Laud today. I sent for da doctor over t' Fair Oaks, but it was too late." She covered her face with her black pudgy hands and sobbed against Amos' shoulder.

Kaitland stood trembling, unable to believe the words from her trusted servant. Her legs felt leaden as she slowly turned and climbed the stairs. Water continued to drip from the beautiful wrap her father had given her for Christmas.

Dulcie swung away from Amos and waddled toward Kaitland, wringing her hands.

"No, honey, you cain't go up der. Please, honey chil', don't go in your Papa's room," she pleaded.

Kaitland moved as if in a daze, impervious to the maid's entreaty, not hearing or seeing anything around her.

"Let her go, Dulcie. She has t' say good-bye."

Kaitland sat in the window seat of her room, her knees drawn up under her chin. She gazed into the black night, monumental responsibilities weighing heavily on her mind.

The rain had stopped and the clouds parted, drawing her vision to a myriad of stars peppering the darkened heavens. Doctor Cubbage had come and gone, declaring in his gruff yet sympathetic manner that Ethan Trevilian had died quickly from a massive stroke.

When she had entered her father's room, he appeared to be only asleep, and she prayed a grave error had been made. As she approached the bed, it had become evident he was dead. The once alive, olive complexion was now blue-gray, the left side of his face drawn into what appeared to be a grimace. She had taken her father's cold hand in hers and wept until there were no more tears.

That was how Doctor Cubbage had found her, and it was only at his insistence that she finally left her father's side. She knew that his keen, observant eye missed little. In his brusque way, he instructed her to get out of her wet clothes and go to bed. There was nothing either of them could do for her father, and he did not want her coming down with pneumonia.

She was alone. The operation of Glen More now fell to her completely. Her father would be proud of her; she would see to that. No matter what it took, she would survive despite the war or whatever else she had to face.

The servants were preparing her father's body for viewing in the parlor. Tomorrow, neighbors from surrounding counties would converge to extend their condolences, bearing enough food to feed half the Confederate Army.

Her vision blurred as hot tears spilled from her already swollen eyes. One part of her wanted to bury, along with her father, this crazy, secret life she had chosen for herself. She was in too deep now. Too many lives depended on her

ability to slip through the night undetected with messages
that could decisively alter the outcome of a major conflict.
No, there was no backing out now. She had made a commitment. To abandon the cause simply because her personal life had become more complicated was not a consideration. The war had forever altered the lives of everyone.
She prayed for strength to carry this awesome obligation.

Kaitland's whispered prayer floated into the silent night
that engulfed her. She moved away from the window, releasing a deep steady breath. Despite her fatigue, a surge
of energy coursed through her. The letter from General
Johnston, still tucked away in her purse, must be delivered. She had given her word. Time was crucial, and she
must go now under the cover of darkness. Tomorrow would
be too risky with so many people descending upon them.

Drawing herself up to her full height, she defiantly raised
a proud chin and began to dress. Her father would have
wanted her to keep her promise to deliver the message.

Kaitland's boots sank into the mud, making walking difficult, as she laboriously made her way to the stable. Amos
was probably asleep now, and since this was a last-minute
decision she did not disturb him. Dulcie might ask too
many questions if she went to their quarters behind the
main house at this hour.

Prince rolled his eyes and pawed the stable floor when
Kaitland first attempted to saddle him, but her calming
voice worked its magic on him. The stallion sidled with
nervousness when she mounted him and whickered a few
times but sensed the determination and steadiness of his
rider and followed her lead.

It started to rain again as she neared the river. The

steadily increasing tempo of pelting icy drops stung her exposed skin. She would be soaked in minutes, but the letter was safe and dry, wrapped in a piece of oiled canvas and tucked in the top of her boot.

Kaitland was forced to slow the mount's pace as he carefully moved through the thick brush and hidden water-filled gullies. The driving deluge obscured the sounds of approaching horses until it was too late. Even though her eyes had become accustomed to the darkness, she could see only a short distance ahead.

Lightening flashed suddenly, illuminating mounted riders several yards to her right. The unexpected light lasted only a split second, but it was long enough to see a Federal patrol. A thunderous roar splintered the monotonous drumming rain, frightening her horse. The animal snorted and neighed, rearing up on his haunches, nearly unseating her. Holding him on a tight rein, his eyes rolling wildly, she gave the horse its head. Perhaps she could outdistance them.

"There he goes, Lieutenant."

"I see him, Sergeant. Pursue and capture. I want him alive."

Kaitland pushed Prince as fast as she dared. Her heart hammered in her breast as her eyes probed the darkness. Hoping to catch sight of her pursuers, she glanced behind her, failing to see a low tree branch in the path. White-hot pain shot through her head as she crashed hard into the limb, her limp body thrown to the ground. That was the last she remembered before blackness engulfed her.

◆

The crisp order given by Christopher Donovan did not re-

flect the fear that knotted his stomach and sent a chill down
his spine. The instant flash of lightening outlined the slight
figure mounted on the stallion from Glen More. There
was no mistaking that horse, and it was unlikely the rider
was a man. With lips compressed into a thin, hard line, he
silently cursed a war that had placed this special woman in
such peril. In his heart, he knew it was Kaitland. How
could he ever arrest her? He found himself wishing for her
escape.

"We got him, Lieutenant. He's down." The sergeant
dismounted near Kaitland's crumpled form lying in the mud
and low brush.

Christopher lunged from his horse before the animal had
stopped, afraid of what he would find.

"Stand aside, Sergeant. I'll take over."

The man stepped back as Christopher frowned darkly
and knelt on one knee beside Kaitland. He gently turned
her over with trembling hands to reveal her mud-streaked
face. The old slouch hat had fallen away, loosening a swath
of red silky strands which lay in the muck.

Christopher's blood froze in his veins. Blood smeared
with mud ran from an abrasion on her forehead. He carefully raised her so her head rested on his leg, his upper
body shielding her from the relentless rain.

"What the—why it's a woman," the astonished sergeant
exclaimed when her hair tumbled over Christopher's supporting arm.

"Yes, it's a woman," Christopher whispered hoarsely,
fumbling under his rain poncho for a handkerchief. With
great care, he attempted to stem the flow of blood from her
wound. It did not seem to be serious, but she was still

unconscious.

"Sergeant, we'll make camp over there under the trees," Christopher ordered tersely, directing the trooper with a wave of his free hand. "Set up a tent if you can in this mess."

"Yes, sir. What do you suppose she's doing out here in the middle of the night?"

Christopher directed his attention to Kaitland, ignoring the soldier's question, trying not to think about the suspicions his men would probably have. He could not blame them for being curious. He felt certain they recognized Kaitland as the woman from Glen More. His reaction to her the day of his search would have been apparent to another man, and they were no doubt wondering how he would handle this whole thing.

"You don't suppose that little slip of a girl could be our spy, do you?" the sergeant said, his question reflecting shock at such an incredulous thought.

"That's what we're here to find out, Sergeant," Christopher snapped.

The soldier's probing only served to increase the anxiety and dread of what he had to do. It went against his grain to interrogate a woman, especially this woman. His men were wet and tired, having been driven with little regard to their needs. He had been like a man possessed given to an unnatural harshness they did not understand. He understood. This small woman he cradled in his arms had shaken him to the very core.

"Carry out my orders, Sergeant."

"Yes, sir."

Christopher directed his attention to the lifeless form leaning against his knee. She looked like a child, peaceful and quiet, oblivious to the chaos around her. "Why you, Kait? Why did it have to be you?" he whispered ardently.

He had not allowed himself time to dwell on how important she had become to him, but he had been unsuccessful in blotting her image from his mind. Now his worst fears were being realized.

Since the dawn of time man had gone off to war, driven by an innate compulsion to conquer. There had always been a cause, an ideology spurred by greed or pride or whatever would justify taking up arms against a foe. While men pursued this quest, innocent victims were inevitably caught in the middle.

This was different. Kaitland was not an enemy on foreign soil whose activities must be thwarted. To him she was an American, a patriot, passionately struggling against what she perceived as an injustice. He was aware of a victorious personality, a resiliency that emanated from her being, invading his thoughts, demanding admiration. Was this part of the faith of which she had spoken? He wondered. Perhaps she was right, he thought wearily. He wasn't sure of anything at this point as he kneeled in three inches of mud with the rain soaking and chilling him to the very marrow of his bones.

He felt as though there were stones in the pit of his stomach. He had always followed orders, doing his duty, proud of his standing as an excellent officer, but his assignment tested his loyalty to the limit. His duty was clear, but his heart was on the brink of challenging an unwavering, unquestioning obedience to the Union directive. Perhaps her God would help him now. Christopher's concentration was broken by his sergeant reporting that a tent had been erected.

"It isn't much, Lieutenant, but it will give you and . . . the lady some protection from the rain."

Christopher ignored the subtle innuendo. "Thank you, Sergeant. You and the men make yourselves as comfortable as possible," he said, lifting Kaitland and carrying her to the tent.

A ground cloth had been laid down in the attempt to create a water-free area in which he could care for her, and the sergeant had left a lighted lantern. With deft gentleness, he bathed her face with water from his canteen. In this crude setting his ministrations were minimal at best. The bleeding had stopped, and she moaned when he touched the bruised flesh.

"Kaitland, can you hear me?"

❧

"Mmmm . . . Christopher?"

Her lashes fluttered, her eyes opening enough to make out the outline and shadows of his face. As consciousness gradually returned, she was able to focus more clearly. She realized her effort to sit up was a mistake, dizziness and pain preventing any sudden movement.

"My head." Through the pounding in her head came the unpleasant odor of wet wool and bone-chilling cold and dampness.

"Just lie still, honey. You're going to have a headache for a while. That's a nasty bump," he said softly, a restraining hand on her shoulder.

She stared into his face, searching for some hint of whether he was aware of the word of endearment he had just used. The memory of being discovered by a patrol flooded through her dulled senses. She had been caught, and Christopher was her captor.

"I must apologize for our lack of appropriate shelter, but I'm certain you are cognizant of the situation," he said with a half hearted grin. His endeavor to inject humor to the obvious lightened the intensity for the moment, evoking a small smile from her. They suddenly felt awkward, even a bit shy, neither one wanting to begin the exchange that was inevitable. The only sounds were the steady drumming of rain on the canvas shelter and the pounding of their hearts.

"Kaitland . . . I . You know what I have to do?"

"I know. You must question me. I understand. I would expect nothing less," she said with a note of acceptance in her voice. Something in the man—an integrity, a sense of duty and a strength that controlled his actions—gave her courage. He would be fair, and that was all she could ask. She had prepared herself for this eventuality, and now the time had come when she must face the consequences for her actions.

She watched him shift his position, sensing the uneasiness he must feel at the prospect of having to drill her. It was an irrefutable decision that must weigh heavily on his heart and mind.

"Are you carrying a message for the Confederacy?" His eyes never wavered from hers, but the question was put with little force, if any.

Poor Christopher. His heart isn't in this, she thought guiltily. It had been her actions that brought them to this desperate impasse. She could not reveal anything voluntarily, and he was a soldier, but just how far will he go? She smiled and asked, "Christopher, have you ever interrogated anyone before?"

"That's not an answer. I expect you—oh, I don't know what I expect." He removed his wet hat and ran his fingers through his damp hair. "What difference does it make?" The frustration he obviously felt evoked a biting edge to his voice.

"None, I suppose." Kaitland set her jaw, and took a deep, steadying breath. "I must answer in the negative."

"Kaitland, surely you don't expect me to believe that."

She raised her chin in the air and with a curt nod, said, "That's all I can tell you."

"Why are you doing this? Don't force me to have you searched." He pleaded with his eyes as much as his voice. "This is very difficult for me. Can't you see that?"

"Christopher, if you discover I am carrying information, will you arrest me?" Her query reflected a tentative sort of awkwardness in her eyes.

"Oh, Kait, I'd give anything to be spared the decision." He sighed heavily and sat down, his arms resting on bent knees. His tall frame seemed to fill the tiny, cramped quarters. She watched the play of emotions. A frowning mixture of desire, loneliness, and frustration crossed his handsome face. The dim light from the single lantern cast shadows across lines of fatigue she had not noticed yesterday. A stubby growth of beard bore evidence he had been in the saddle too long with little care for himself. Why was he driving himself and his men so hard?

She hated this position into which he had been forced. She cared for him more than she was willing to admit.

This dilemma was tearing him apart. Her admiration for him at this moment was boundless. His integrity and his devotion to duty were in direct conflict with his personal feelings. She had thought of him as a formidable adversary when they first met. She no longer felt that way.

The dizziness had subsided, so she sat up and placed her hand on his arm. "Christopher, I know the evidence is damning. Any fool can see a woman dressed as I am, riding alone in a rainstorm could have only one reason for doing so. Please don't berate yourself for being what you are."

He watched her in silence for a moment. "Do you know I could lose myself in those incredibly gentle eyes of yours? Despite your dire circumstances, I can't find a trace of fear in your lovely face; only serenity and peace. How can you be so forgiving?" He took her in the circle of his arms and kissed her desperately, longingly, like a dying man clinging to life.

Kaitland melted into the safety of his embrace, a shiver of expectancy trembling over the softness of her lips. She had felt so utterly alone when her father died, but for this precious moment Christopher filled that void, providing sustenance to her starving spirit.

Rifle fire suddenly pierced through the steady staccato of rain thudding against the small tent. Then they heard another shot and the shouts of frantic men. Frenzied mayhem surrounded them within seconds. Several frightening screams broke through the confusion. They could only be those of Confederate soldiers who had become known for their bloodcurdling, unnerving shrieks, identified as the rebel yell.

Christopher stiffened, instinctively reaching for the Colt army revolver holstered at his side. "Wait here and stay low."

The special moment they had shared was gone, destroyed once again by the war. He scrambled out of the tent before she could respond.

Wait here? Did he honestly expect her to remain in the middle of a skirmish? The first few moments of confusion passed quickly. She crawled to the tent opening, cautiously peeking into the gray light of early morning. The rain had abated somewhat, and patches of fog hugged the ground.

Christopher's men were running in all directions seeking cover from the scattered, well-hidden rebel soldiers. Their numbers were indeterminable. Many Confederate troops fought with unconventional tactics, thereby confusing the enemy.

She searched the area for Christopher, but she could not see him anywhere. There were horses picketed a few yards away, Prince tied along with them. Her only chance for escape was now, while the men were occupied with saving their own lives.

She piled her muddy, wet hair on top of her head and pulled on the worn hat. Her head began to pound from the exertion, and she wondered if she would ever feel clean and dry again. The only dry thing on her was probably the message still concealed in her boot.

Kaitland crawled toward the horses, sinking into freezing mud, briars pricking her tender flesh. Fortunately, the fighting seemed to be on the other side of the hastily made camp. She untied the reins of her horse and cautiously walked him away from the camp and into the brush.

Slight dizziness blurred her vision, slowing her progress, but she managed to swing into the saddle and urge Prince in the direction she hoped to find Tim. She uttered a silent prayer he had not moved far from his last position. She knew she could ride long in her present condition.

Shivers shook her body with every movement, and dull pain wracked each nerve in her head. Still she continued to push through the woodlands that had been transformed into soft, miry mud. If it were not for the stamina of her stallion, the quest would have been impossible.

She thought of Christopher. The few moments they had shared were so very special. She had felt the inner conflict which had tormented him as he held her in his arms. Was he safe at this minute? Had he been—No. She would not dwell on the dangers he faced.

Why was she not concerned about the rebels engaged in the battle? Those were the men she should be worrying about and she did, but what would Christopher do when he found out she had escaped?

"Halt! Pull up there, or I'll shoot."

The command tore through the air like a shot. Suddenly a man appeared, emerging from a clump of tall brush just ahead. Why did that voice sound so familiar?

She stopped, feeling too ill for fear to have its usual effect.

"Okay. Now, git off o' that animal and keep your hands in clear view."

"Corporal Beamer, it's Kaitland Trevilian. Remember me? I spoke to Lieutenant Carrington several days ago," she said, grateful at last to have reached the end of her journey. Time was running out. Having been caught by

Christopher had taken valuable time and it would be impossible to return home before sunup now.

"Well, I'll be switched if it ain't the gal spy." The bedraggled guard approached Kaitland, a broad grin revealing stained, widely spaced teeth through his scruffy beard.

"I s'pose you want to see—" Suddenly his brow furrowed, shock plain on his face. He came closer to her and stared openmouthed at her disheveled appearance.

"Good Lord, Miss Trevilian. What happened? Your head!"

"It's a long story, Corporal. I ran into a Federal patrol, but managed to escape. I must see Lieutenant Carrington immediately. It's urgent." She could feel herself growing weaker and prayed Tim was not far away.

"Yes, ma'am. I'll take you right away, but it's cap'n now. Lieutenant Carrington got hisself a promotion," the soldier said proudly. "He's one fine man. Yes sir, one fine man."

"Yes, I know, Corporal. Could we go now?"

"Yes, ma'am. You jist sit there on that black monster of yours, and I'll lead you right to the cap'n's doorstep."

The corporal started through the trees, continuing a one-sided conversation. Kaitland was too tired and weak to respond.

"Guess that's a tent step in this case." He chuckled. "Yes, ma'am, we had ourselves a few rounds with them Yankees and done ourselves proud too. The cap'n said all his men was gittin' promotions. Ain't that somethin'? Gittin' a promotion for jist knockin' off a few Yankees. Why, I'd adone that for nothin'," he said, spitting a disgusting blob of dark-brown tobacco juice on the ground.

His voice droned on while Kaitland struggled to stay in the saddle. The rain had stopped, but the air was damp and heavy, and she was chilled to the bone. Her mind began wandering to the past with its bright sunny days, long rides with her father—

"Kaitland! Where in the world did you come from?"

How did she arrive in Tim's camp without realizing where she was?

"I found her headin' right for us, Cap'n. She don't look too good either. Had a blow on the head and was took by some Yankees and then escaped."

"Thank you, Corporal. I'll see to her," Tim answered, lifting Kaitland from the horse and gently setting her down. "Take care of her horse."

"Yes, sir. I'll do that. That little gal could use some vittles if you ask me," he said, leading the big stallion to a picket line.

"Is he right, Kaitland? Has all that happened to you?" Tim observed her critically.

"I'm afraid so, but some of our men attacked the patrol, and I was able to sneak away." She sighed tiredly.

"Maybe so, but you don't look well." Tim cupped her cheek with his hand, his eyes boring into hers. "You have a fever, and your head is badly bruised."

"Tim, I'll be fine as soon as I can get home to a hot bath. I have a message from General Johnston. Can you deliver it to General Hill or find someone who can?"

"A.P. Hill? That may take some doing," he said thoughtfully. "He's constantly on the move, but I'll find him. When did you see General Johnston and why?"

"I went to Richmond yesterday to tell him I'd heard that

McClellan planned the invasion on the York River. He asked me to deliver a message to anyone who could find General Hill. I naturally thought of you."

She bent down and retrieved the carefully guarded letter from the top of her boot. When she stood up again, a wave of nausea flowed over her and the world spun out of focus.

Tim caught her as she swayed, her knees buckling, then carried her to his tent. With infinite care he laid her on his cot.

"Tim, I must go home," she whispered.

"Shh. You're in no condition to go anywhere." He dipped a cloth in water and placed it on her forehead.

"Tim, you don't understand." A tear slid from beneath her closed eyes. "Papa died yesterday." A choked sob caught in her throat.

"Oh, Kait, I'm sorry."

She slowly raised her gaze to meet the sorrow she saw in Tim's eyes. He had known her father all of his life, and the news of his death was hard for him, too. He was quiet for several moments, sitting beside her on an ammunition box. He rubbed the back of his neck in an agitated motion and stared at the wet ground.

"What happened?" he asked softly, holding her hand.

"He suffered a stroke and passed away quickly while I was in Richmond." Kaitland chewed her lip, making an effort to hold back the tears threatning to spill from her watery eyes. Her nerves were strung taut. The events of the past few days had brought her to the point of complete exhaustion.

"He was a fine man and a gentleman, Kait. I'm deeply sorry. What . . . what will you do now?" A characteristic small frown creased his handsome brow.

She knew what he meant. How would she manage alone with no family to help her? "Tim, women all over the South are running farms and plantations alone while their men serve in the army. I can manage as well. I've learned a great deal since Papa became ill, and I'm certain to learn much more by trial and error."

"You need a foreman, someone who can take the responsibility of the crops and the stock." He stood up, his head nearly touching the highest point in the confining tent. "I wish I were available to help . . . to be near . . . maybe—"

"Tim, we've been through this before."

"I know, but the situation has changed. Oh, blast it all, Kait. You know I'm in love with you." He sat down beside her again, taking her hands in his. "Marry me, Kait. I can take care of you and Glen More. My father will send some of our men to help you while I'm away. You shouldn't be riding all over the county, nearly getting yourself killed. Say 'yes' and I'll . . ." His voice faded away as he studied her expression. Suddenly he stood and turned away from her, thrusting his hands in his trouser pockets.

"Who is it, Kaitland?"

"Tim, I don't—"

"There's someone else. I see it in your eyes. Who is it? I want to know who I've lost out to. Is it someone I know?"

Was there someone? Someone for whom she felt strongly, but refused to acknowledge? There could be only one person who stirred such emotion in her, who brought every nerve in her body alive with desire. How could she tell Tim it was a Federal officer who had turned her world upside down? "Yes, there is someone, but his name isn't important.

"Tim, I would give anything if I could say yes to your proposal, but it would never work for us. One day you would resent me for taking the easy way out and using you. I couldn't do that to you." It hurt to see the pain and disappointment flicker in his blue eyes.

He managed a bitter smile.

"I hope he knows what a lucky man he is. All right," he said resignedly, taking a deep breath. "I'll take you home. I know this area better than you. Can you sit in a saddle?"

"I think so, but you don't have to take me. Don't you need to stay here?" Her head still hurt when she sat up, but the dizziness was gone.

"It won't take long," he said, helping her from the cot. "You must have circled around more than you realize. We're only a few miles from Glen More."

"But the message should be delivered." She leaned against Tim's strong supporting body, his arm around her waist.

"I won't be away long enough for it to matter one way or the other. I should be able to find Hill by tomorrow morning at the latest. Now stop worrying. You've done your part, and it's time we got you home, young lady."

six

"Now, honey chil', you jist rest and empty dat perdy head o' everything. Ol' Dulcie gonna take care of them folks down in da parlor."

The Negro servant fluttered about the room, and after tucking clean sheets around Kaitland, she picked up the tray of half-eaten food from the small rosewood bed table.

"Thank you, Dulcie. Please explain and offer my regrets. I'm sure Mrs. Pettibone is here, and she will no doubt take charge. She can be a bit overbearing, but she ... means well."

The county busybody from a neighboring plantation rushed to Kaitland's aid as soon as the news of Ethan's death reached her. She gave orders like a drill sergeant, but possessed a knack for accomplishing the impossible and organizing any affair.

Kaitland's speech was slurred, barely above a whisper. A small draught had been added to her tea as Doctor Cubbage had ordered. He was still in the area delivering a baby when Amos had again summoned him to Glen More. Tim had brought her to the back entrance of the main house to avoid inquisitive eyes. Neighbors had already begun arriving as he discreetly kept her out of sight.

"Yes, 'um. Dat woman have a way o' handlin' folks," Dulcie said, chuckling. She stroked Kaitland's brow lovingly. "Jist you rest now, honey. Ain't nobody gonna bother you wid ol' Dulcie 'round."

Kaitland felt weightless and relaxed, her body seemingly floating on air. The persistent headache had lessened, and if she kept her eyes closed, the sickening dizziness could be kept at bay. Dulcie had bathed and dressed her as she had done many times when Kaitland was a child. She had remained quiet during the old woman's fussing, enduring the orders given incessantly to her two granddaughters who helped with the household chores. Dulcie had been mumbling throughout the entire procedure about the evils of women riding alone, especially on a wild horse such as that black devil.

Tim's only explanation had been that he had found Kaitland after she had fallen from her horse, striking her head on a rock. *Bless you, Tim,* she thought as she drifted into a peaceful slumber. His story would explain her present condition, and no one need ever know why she had been out riding. Considering her father's sudden death and her reputation for doing the unexpected, few would question her actions. They would attribute her behavior to grief.

⁂

Silence fell over the gathering on the first floor with its low hum of respectful voices when someone shouted, "Yankees! Yankees comin' down the road!"

Christopher raised his hand and brought to a halt the thundering beat of his men's horses galloping in a double-file column. The air was heavy with the rank odor of lathered horses, wet leather, and men who had been deprived of personal hygiene for too long.

He watched a portly gentleman with florid apple-red cheeks and an expression akin to that of a bulldog descend the porch steps. The older man assumed a stance and air of bravado that did not surprise Christopher. He had seen the indignant, defiant pose from several Southern sympathizers.

He knew his appearance and that of his men was nothing short of disgraceful, but he didn't care. He was exhausted, dirty, and unshaven, but more to the point was the smoldering anger ready to erupt at the slightest provocation. He hoped keeping it under control would not prove to be an exercise in futility.

Above the jangle of metal bits and grunting horses, Christopher had no difficulty in making himself heard. The formality of introductions and the niceties of protocol were abandoned as his attention bore down on the man standing before him. Somehow he did not fit the image he had of Kaitland's father. She had indicated he was in poor health, but he did not appear to be ill.

"Mr. Trevilian, I must ask you to stand aside. It is imperative that I speak with your daughter," Christopher said harshly. He was not certain what, if anything, he hoped to resolve by this visit to Glen More. Perhaps under the guise of official military business he wanted to satisfy himself that she was all right.

The old man has nerve, he thought. He has not shown any sign of backing down. But, he did not expect him to. He exemplified the attitude of the South and the Confederacy.

"It is apparent you have no idea to whom you are speaking, suh. Haven't you wondered why there are so many carriages on the grounds? Mr. Trevilian died yesterday, and I, suh, am Jasper Monroe. I will determine who visits

Miss Trevilian and who does not. This household is in mourning, so I must ask you to leave with utmost haste."

Christopher had noticed the number of buggies and horses on the grounds, but did not give the reason much thought. The death of her father was a shock, even a complication, but his single-minded directive to see Kaitland would not be deterred. He was now even more anxious to see her. He had been infuriated when he found she had escaped, but his concern for her safety now overshadowed his wrath.

"I'm deeply sorry to learn of Mr. Trevilian's passing. I naturally assumed you were he since we had never met. My mission, however, cannot be altered at this point. I regret the intrusion, but I will speak to Miss Trevilian. My business is official and urgent."

"I can't imagine what business a Yankee officer could have with Kaitland. She is a loyal Confederate," Mr. Monroe said forcefully, hooking his thumbs in his velvet vest pockets. "She does not entertain the enemy."

Christopher ignored the man's statement and swung down from his trail weary horse, handing the reins to his sergeant. "Sergeant, dismount and let the men rest. I won't be long."

Brushing past the corpulent gentleman, Christopher climbed the steps determinedly, an inner force driving him on.

"Now see here, Lieutenant. You can't just barge in here at a time like this. Have you no respect? I'll not stand for it."

The blustering man followed Christopher into the house, attempting to dissuade this invasion of privacy. "Miss Trevilian is confined to her bed, poor dear. She is suffer-

ing from fatigue and a concussion sustained when she fell
from her horse. You must not disturb her."

Without the support of more men, his tone had changed
considerably. Most of the callers this early in the day were
women, and they had hidden themselves behind closed
doors.

Christopher stopped and turned to face the flustered old
man. He sighed with weariness and impatience, rubbing
his eyes with the back of his hand.

"Sir, I am wet, hungry, and bone tired—too weary to
argue with you. I am saddened to learn of Mr. Trevilian's
death. I am equally saddened by Miss Trevilian's delicate
state of health at this time, and I do respect her privacy. It
is with my deepest apology, however, that I must insist
upon seeing her alone. Now, I can go up the stairs and
look in each room until I find her, or you can direct me. It
matters not at all how we do this."

The asperity with which he had spoken was increased
by his thinly contolled patience and his voice rose to a
crescendo.

"In her bedchamber? My good man, surely you don't
expect me to allow you to see her alone in there?" Mr.
Monroe dabbed perspiration from his brow and nervously
extracted a silver cigar case from his coat pocket.

"The fact that she is ill would seem to dictate in which
room I would find her. We're wasting time, sir. Shall we
go?" Christopher began to climb the wide stairs, oblivious that his mud-spattered boots were leaving tracks on
the plush carpet. Mr. Monroe was right behind him. At
the top of the stairs, Christopher stopped, and the older
man stepped in front of him.

"I'll wait outside the door. I trust you will conduct your-self as a gentleman," he said, clearly resigned to the situation.

"Of course."

"The doctor said she needed rest." Mr. Monroe sighed heavily and gestured toward Kaitland's room. "It gives me no pleasure to give in to a Yankee, sir, but I realize the futility of trying to thwart your determined stand."

Christopher nodded and pushed open the door. He stood for a moment on the threshold to allow his eyes to adjust to the meager light. The room was in semidarkness, the heavy drapes having been drawn, but low-burning embers in the fireplace cast a warm glow about the interior. The faint fragrance of lavender drifted on the air, and Christopher suddenly felt very much an interloper in the feminine surroundings.

His eyes fell on the slight figure asleep on the canopied bed, and his ire fled. A yellow glow from a chimney candle on the bedside commode illuminated her pale face. He moved to stand by her bed and was struck by the delicate beauty so evident in her still and undisturbed state. He was captivated by her soft pale skin, and sensitive mouth turned up at the corners as if ready to smile. He had never seen hair the color of hers. Flickering light from the candle shimmered and danced on the red-gold strands changing the red to russet. Then he noticed the small dressing on her forehead. Pain seized and twisted his gut as he remembered his emotional turmoil when he had held her limp wet body earlier that day.

For a moment his heart faltered with trepidation, but then he saw the slight rising and falling of her chest and was able to breathe again.

"Oh, Kait, why can't you be like other women and do whatever it is women do?" he whispered fervently. He realized she was so special because she was not like other women. He knelt beside the bed and took her small hand in his. He wanted to commit this moment to memory, this picture of her imprinted on his mind that he might draw strength from it later.

⋅⋟⋅

Kaitland slowly returned to consciousness with a disquieting awareness that she was not alone. She moaned softly in weak protest as she moved into the realm of acute discomfort. Her whole body ached as if she had been cruelly beaten and abused.

Her eyes fluttered open. She was astonished for a moment. "Have you come to arrest me?" she whispered hoarsely through a weak smile.

"I have nothing to charge you with, remember? I have only my suspicions and circumstantial evidence," he said gently, drinking in every detail of her expression. "You're a formidable adversary, pretty lady."

She considered his words thoughtfully. Did he still think of her as an adversary?

"How do you feel?" His smile changed to a frown of concern, further creasing his strained features.

"Oh, it'll take more than a little bump on the head to keep me down." The weak attempt to make light of her condition obviously did not fool him.

"Maybe, but you're awfully pale. You took a terrible spill from that demon you ride. You could have been killed."

"You don't look so well yourself, Lieutenant." Her smile

faded. "Christopher, the skirmish . . . I . . ."

"I lost two men." He looked down at her hand clasped in his. Unconsciously, he made little circular motions on her wrist with his thumb. "I think Johnny Reb got away without a scratch, though." He looked back at her with a disarming smile. "Your boys in gray can be a crafty lot, Kait, my dear."

She searched his face, but did not find the mockery she might have expected. She accepted his statement as he must have intended. It was a genuine compliment on the skill of the Confederate soldier. The death of his men had obviously affected him more deeply than anyone could have imagined. His eyes mirrored such sadness and regret.

A muscle twitched in Christopher's jaw. "Kait, I still have to ask you a few questions. I hate myself for pushing you, adding to your problems at a time like this, but my report to command must reflect that proper procedures have been followed." He rubbed his forehead with his hand and closed his eyes. He fell silent for a few moments, then ground out between clinched teeth, his eyes still closed. "I hate this war. It's ripping apart the lives of so many people."

Finally, he looked up and took a halting breath, "Why did you leave, Kait?"

She frowned slightly, considering her answer. "If you had been in my, shall we say, somewhat questionable position, would you have stayed?"

"I guess not. Even so, you know I have to ask. Our relationship is rather unusual, wouldn't you say?"

"Yes I would, but we were interrupted before you answered my question. If you had found that I was carrying surreptitiously acquired information, would you have arrested me?"

There was a curious dark flame in his eyes, and she tried to assess the play of emotions that crossed his tired face. He suddenly stood up and began pacing the floor. Despite the frustrations and doubts that apparently haunted him, he was still a man in absolute control of himself.

"Kaitland, this is no game we're playing. It's serious military business, and I'm under direct orders, but my personal feelings for you keep getting in the way."

He came back and knelt beside her again, his eyes fixed on hers. "Lady, you're very special to me. Can't you stop giving me cause to watch and to follow you? You could remove me from the position of having to make that decision if you just give up these activities."

The agony in his plea tugged at her heart, releasing a flood of compassion for this man who had complicated yet completed her life. She touched his face and whispered, "Christopher, we cannot ask the impossible of each other. I cannot ask you to disobey your orders, and I cannot make any promises."

He took her hand and kissed her palm, his eyes closed. "I'm trying to understand, Kait. I had hoped to resolve the impasse we've reached. Perhaps you're right," he murmured tiredly.

The inner force which drove him—the passion and fierceness where this assignment was concerned seemed to drain away from him. She hated to see him look so defeated.

"My report will read that I was unable to substantiate my suspicions, and without sufficient evidence an arrest had become impossible. There are no other options.

"I must leave now. Mr. Monroe made it clear that you

needed rest, and I agree. I expect him to charge in here any minute and have me removed by the seat of my pants."

They both smiled at the unlikelihood of that happening.

"He's probably pacing the hall, chewing savagely on one of his Havana cigars that he prizes so highly. I was always so happy Papa never filled the house with that disgusting stench."

"Kait, I'm sorry about your father. I wish that under different circumstances I could have known him."

"So do I. You would have liked him, I think." Her eyes filled with tears.

"Why didn't you tell me this morning?"

She looked away as a tear escaped, tracing a path to her hair. A sob caught in her throat as she spoke. "So many other things crowded in . . . I . . . "

"I know. I know," he said softly and kissed her forehead. "Will you be all right? I mean alone. I know your father had been ill for sometime and hadn't been much help, but now the full weight of responsibility for this place falls on you."

With his index finger under her chin, Christopher turned her head to face him. He smiled and said, "Where's all that fire and spirit, huh? Where is that strength and faith you told me about?"

Kaitland's face brightened. He was trying so hard to sound lighthearted and casual. "Oh, it's there. It just needs bolstering occasionally."

A weak but charming smile brought a glow to her delicate features. "That's my girl." He chuckled.

"I hope my presence here today hasn't irreparably damaged the sensitivity of your neighbors. I think they expected me to have two heads and to be breathing fire."

"They just don't know you're more bark than bite."
There was a teasing note in her voice.

"Take care, Kait." He bent over and touched her lips
with a feathery kiss, then turned to leave.

"Christopher, wait." Kaitland raised herself enough to
open a small drawer in the table by her bed. She extracted
a small worn Testament that had been her mother's. She
held it for a moment, caressing its soft leather cover before
turning her thoughts to what she was about to do. It felt
right. Christopher should have it.

"I want you to have this. Will you carry it and maybe
read from it when you have a quiet moment to yourself?"
she asked hesitantly.

He stood unmoving for so long she thought he was going
to refuse the offer. Then he slowly reached out and took
the Testament. He stared at it, but said nothing. His eyes
remained fixed on the book, and he was obviously moved.
Kaitland realized his hesitation had not been caused by
resentment, but by a complexity of emotions she could not
describe.

"It was my mother's, and I think she would have wanted
you to have it. It would make me very happy if you would
accept it."

He placed the Testament in his shirt pocket, buttoning
the flap. "Thank you, Kait. I'll carry it with me, and I
will read it. Perhaps I'll find something of what you have
in your life. It having been your mother's makes it a very
special gift. Are you sure?"

"Yes, I'm sure."

Then he was gone.

A tear slid from the corner of her eye into the softness of her hair. How long would it be before she saw him again? The alternative was unthinkable. She closed her eyes tightly against the insidious effects of the war.

❧

Christopher mounted his horse and rode the muddy road from Glen More, his mind bombarded with a tangle of emotions commanding all of his attention. No one had ever given him anything that meant as much to him. She must care a great deal to give him such a treasured possession. Until this moment he had not been certain, had not wanted to believe what was now so clear. There was no longer any doubt. He was in love with this beautiful creature who was driving him crazy with her daring spirit and commitment to a cause that would bring her nothing but more heartbreak. That was part of what had been tearing him apart for days. He knew she would not give up this private war she waged.

seven

Ethan Trevilian was buried next to his wife in the family cemetery on a knoll several hundred yards from the main house. The small plot was well cared for, landscaped with crepe myrtle and English boxwood. An ornately designed iron fence encircled the final resting place of Trevilians.

Kaitland remained at the graveside long after Pastor Glidden completed the service. Friends and neighbors had either returned home or had gone to the house. It was customary for friends to remain with the family for a time to give support and lend assistance should immediate problems arise due to a sudden death. In this instance, Kaitland would simply pick up where she had left off. The loss of her father was profound, but she was happy he had at last found peace and was with his Adeline. She was also grateful he would never see the devastation of the war that crept ever closer to Glen More. That would have killed him if the stroke had not.

"Child, it's time you returned to the house."

Mrs. Pettibone put her arm around Kaitland's shoulders and guided her away from the open grave. She did not resist the woman's gentle urging. She had said her goodbyes the night he died.

Four slaves were standing at a discreet distance, shovels ready, waiting for Kaitland to leave. She had requested the grave not be covered until she had left. To hear the thud of dirt clods falling on her father's coffin would be more than she could bear.

"Yes, thank you, Mrs. Pettibone. You've been very helpful. I must thank you for arranging everything so well. It would have been difficult for me."

"No thanks are necessary, my dear. I was only too happy to help out. How are you feeling? Is the dizziness gone?"

"Yes. A couple of days of rest was all I needed," Kaitland said noncommittally. She was certain the woman had hoped for more information about why she had gone riding in such foul weather. Christopher's visit was the talk of the county, but no one had imposed on her bereavement with questions.

"Well, I hope you'll be more careful in the future about traipsing off alone. A woman shouldn't be out alone these days, especially with those terrible Yankees roaming all over this country. Imagine, riding right to your front door and demanding to see you and your papa not yet cold. It's disgraceful."

Kaitland winced from the unthinking remark.

"Oh, I'm sorry, Kaitland. I shouldn't have said that. Anyway, as I was saying, you were mighty fortunate that handsome young Tim Carrington found you and . . ."

The nasal, high-pitched voice droned on, words enunciated with such rapidity Kaitland felt certain the woman's tongue would drop off from exhaustion.

She smiled and nodded, but her mind drifted to more pleasant memories of her father and Christopher. Christopher. How she wished circumstances were such that he could be here with her now.

A gust of chilling wind whipped the black skirts of the

women as they hurried to the house. The sky had become overcast with thick low clouds threatening rain again. Absently, Kaitland wondered about spring planting. If this wet weather persisted, crops would be late this year.

For the next few weeks, citizens of the peninsula between the James and York Rivers were in the midst of General McClellan's steady advance toward Richmond. General Johnston continued to fall back against the relentless onslaught of heavy artillery and engineering. McClellan's goal was the capture of Richmond, the Confederate capitol. The success of this endeavor would bring the Confederacy to her knees and a swift end to the war.

Heavy rains continued through early May, day after dreary day. The Federal Army with its enormous amount of supplies and equipment were constantly being bogged down in the mud. Many bloody battles took place during the spring months and into early summer with casualties heavy on both sides. At one time the Federal Army came within seven miles of Richmond, but was repulsed. As Confederate troops were driven back toward the Capitol, General Johnston was wounded and replaced by General Lee.

It was during this period that Kaitland had become graphically aware of what war really meant in terms of human sacrifice.

A steady stream of wagons, horses, ambulances, and weary men from both armies traveled the road near Glen More. It was a rare day when assistance was not requested from the large plantation by one army or the other. At times she could hear heavy artillery fire thundering in the distance. Several encounters were fought within a few miles of Glen More. Flashes from cannon and artillery fire set the night sky ablaze like a thousand fireworks, but there was nothing to celebrate now.

Kaitland fell into bed each night completely spent. The overwhelming demands on her time of keeping the plantation running smoothly and aiding soldiers as they passed by were awesome. She could not turn her back on any wounded man, regardless of which army he served. She managed to supply whatever was asked to the extent of depleting her own reserves. And the rain—would it never stop?

"Miz Kaitlan', is you gonna help dem Yankee soldiers again?" Amos asked one miserably wet day in early June.

"Yes, Amos. We'll give aid to anyone who needs it. I doubt that offering a little comfort to these men will turn the tide of the war." She continued sorting old sheets and instructing some women field hands in preparing hot food to be taken to the barn.

It was apparent that Amos was confused by her blind assistance. She claimed to support the Confederacy, yet she aided the enemy whenever he came to her. The decision had been made so simple. Every time she witnessed a suffering young Union soldier, Christopher's face seemed to be before her eyes.

She hadn't seen or heard from him since the day he had come to her room. This was not surprising, considering the major campaign that was underway. He had probably been reassigned. The command undoubtedly needed his expertise elsewhere since the capture of Richmond was more important than the apprehension of one spy, especially one who could not be caught in the act.

Every night she prayed for his safety. The one indisputable fact that tormented her every waking minute was that if anything happened to him, she would never know. His family would be notified, but she doubted they knew of her existence. He had not talked much about his relatives.

Endless hours of hard work were a balm to hours of sagging spirits and depressing thoughts. There was no time to dwell on the unthinkable possibility she might never see him again. She worked from sunup until well past midnight, and the few hours of sleep she managed to squeeze into the dreadful schedule were deep and dreamless.

As Kaitland folded the last sheet, an ambulance pulled up and stopped in the drive. The sergeant in charge jumped down, requesting permission to use her barn as a shelter for the night. The heavy rains had made it impossible for them to reach the field hospital before dark. The wounded might not survive a night in the rain.

She had helped care for numerous wounded men in recent weeks, but she was unprepared for the pitiful heap of humanity she found in the barn that night.

As she entered, the stench was the first indication of what she faced. Swallowing a wave of nausea that seized her, she raised the lantern higher as though its light would help dispel the demons of war. Amos followed behind carrying several lanterns which he hung on the walls, instantly illuminating the figures of twelve men. The two ambulance drivers stood up when they entered. Ten wounded men were lying on dry straw pallets.

"Ma'am, we're mighty grateful for your hospitality. I hope we haven't put you out too much." The sergeant in charge stepped forward. His uniform was barely recognizable beneath a thick crust of mud. Sweat and blood had stained the ill-fitting coat long before the more recent mud splatters.

"Not at all, Sergeant. Amos has hot stew for those who are able to eat. I brought chicken broth for the more seriously wounded. I'm sorry we can't offer you coffee, but it's become difficult to find."

"Thanks, ma'am. A hot meal sounds real good." The sergeant moved to help Amos while the other driver went to assist those patients who could feed themselves.

"Sergeant, would it be all right if I cleaned and dressed some of their wounds?" she said hesitantly. "I have clean bandages for them."

There had been stories circulating about soldiers who had taken advantage of many Southerners by returning their kindness with acts of robbery and pillage, especially when they found a woman alone. Worse yet, they heard that some Confederates were found stealing from their own people.

"Oh, yes, ma'am. That would be just fine. Some of these boys ain't had much done for them since the battle of Grapevine Bridge two days ago."

Kaitland suspected this sort of neglect occurred often in the confusion of battle retreats and advances. The man exhibited little concern for his comrades' misery.

Three days indeed. No wonder the odor was overpowering. She set about her task with determination and at the same time fighting to control the ever-present threat of retching.

One young man, a boy of about sixteen, had sustained abdominal and head wounds. It was a miracle he was still alive and conscious. After removing the bloody bandage from his stomach, it took all of her will to continue looking at the boy. The wound had become putrid, alive with maggots. His eyes were glazed, his dirty face contorted with pain, but he made no sound other than his ragged gurgling breathing.

As Kaitland gingerly cleaned the wound as best she could, the boy stared at her with large trusting eyes and murmured haltingly, "Thank you, ma'am."

"What's your name, son?" she asked, even though he wasn't much younger than she.

"Tommy Simpson, ma'am." In a voice barely above a hoarse whisper, managing a faint smile, he spoke with great effort through cracked feverish lips, "Am I gonna die? I don't feel so good."

"I don't know, Tommy, but I'll try to help you."

Kaitland smiled through hot tears that gathered, burning her eyes. It didn't take a doctor to see this poor boy would probably never live through the night.

"I'd be honored if you would call me Kaitland." With tender care she covered the hideous gaping hole in Tommy's middle. There was little else she could do for him. "Tommy, I'm going to help the other men, and then I'll be back. Could you swallow a little broth?"

"I'll try, ma'am . . . Kaitland. Don't be long, please," the boy croaked.

Kaitland turned her head to hide the tears as she gathered up meager supplies. The painful pleading in this brave lad's face and the senselessness of his suffering began to shred her convictions about the war. This scene was no doubt being repeated hundreds of times in battle after battle throughout several states. Children were fighting for a cause they probably didn't understand. The axiom of this war—the confidence of Southerners believing that all wrongs would somehow be transformed into right—was becoming more elusive with each passing day.

Kaitland did what she could for the other men, none of whom seemed to be in a life-threatening situation, but all were in need of clean dressings. The prolonged delay in receiving treatment was taking its toll, however. They would not survive if professional care was not administered soon. It seemed tragic that men who fought bravely must die because of too little care too late.

When she finally was able to get back to Tommy, it was immediately evident that his condition was deteriorating rapidly.

"How do you feel, Tommy?" she asked softly, bathing his forehead with a cool cloth.

He didn't answer right away. "Not too good. Kaitland, would you write to my ma and tell her where I am? I . . . I ran away and joined the army. She's probably real worried."

"Of course, Tommy." She sent Amos off to bring pen and paper. It was the very least she could do for the dying boy, and it might help to ease his mother's grief to know he wasn't alone when death had come.

She wrote down the necessary information with the brief message he dictated between painful pauses as he struggled to gather enough strength to continue. She would add a note herself later when her thoughts were clearer.

"Kaitland, it hurts. It hurts real bad."

The barn was still except for the irregular ragged breath-

ing of the boy as he clung to life. The other men were all
too familiar with the gruesome sounds.

"I know, Tommy. Here, hold my hand, tightly." She
took his cold, dirty hand between hers, absorbing the trem-
ors that continually rippled through his dying body.

"You won't leave, will ya, Kaitland?" he asked through
clenched teeth, panic showing in his youthful eyes. His
body began to tremble more violently, whether from the
cold or the pain she was unsure, but she covered him with
her cloak.

"No, I promise not to leave you." She moved closer to
him, hoping to transmit some of her body warmth. His
lips were so blue.

"Tommy, do you ever pray?"

"Sometimes. Ma took us kids to church a lot. I believe
in the Almighty." He was gasping for breath now, making
speech more difficult.

"I'm glad. Don't try to talk anymore. Just concentrate
on the good things you remember about your home. Think
about your mother and those things that give you pleasure
and joy, your brothers and sisters and the fun you had together."

Kaitland smoothed his feverish brow and brushed the
brown curls away from his closed eyes. He was so young
and innocent, she thought. He would never see adulthood
or taste the joy of just being alive and taking his place in
the world.

"Miz Kaitland, ain't you goin' back t' da house?" Amos
stood behind her, obviously concerned about her staying
here with these men.

"No, Amos. I promised to stay with this boy. Oh, Amos,

he's just a child. Look at him."

"Yes, 'um. Dat he is."

"I'll be all right. I can't leave him now. I doubt he has long." She sighed releasing a slow shaky breath. "No one should die alone."

"No, 'um. He be mighty young t' meet da Laud. I 'spect it'll help da boy if you stay with him." Amos sat down on a pile of straw near Kaitland and silently waited with her.

Tommy Simpson slipped into unconsciousness and died quietly within the hour. Kaitland held his hand long after the gasping breaths ceased and life ebbed away from the young stranger. Her prayer for his release from pain had been answered. Before the end, his pain-filled grimace had eased, and he became peaceful, no longer aware of his body's agony.

As she left the barn she asked the sergeant if there would be any objection to Tommy Simpson being buried at Glen More.

"Well, that'd be mighty nice of you, ma'am. The boy deserves a decent buryin'."

She got the distinct impression the sergeant was relieved to have the responsibility taken from him.

"We'll be leavin' by first light, ma'am. Thanks again for your kindness."

"You're welcome, Sergeant."

Kaitland found sleep elusive despite the ever-present fatigue. Each time she closed her eyes she saw Tommy's face, then gradually it faded, and Christopher's image replaced the lad's haunting eyes. The realization that Christopher could be on some bloodstained battlefield, seriously wounded or worse turned the drowsy thoughts into a living nightmare.

There seemed to be no end in sight to the fighting. Even though the advance to capture Richmond was proving to be futile, the Federals were not inclined to give up. The battles were fierce and casualties mounted into the thousands.

One battle particularly close to Glen More had left Kaitland fearful and edgy. Heavy artillery sending thunderous mortar shells screaming toward the enemy had pierced through her head like painful darts. She had lain in her bed that night listening to the shells whirring in the distance, feeling the ground rumble beneath her. She closed her eyes tightly and covered her ears with her hands in a frantic effort to block out the nerve-wracking memory. It had been close. Too close. She wondered how many more times the fighting would be that near to Glen More before the end.

As the first streaks of dawn sent long fingers of charcoal gray light across her room, Kaitland heard the ambulances leaving. The sound of creaking wagons and plodding mules moving slowly through the mud drifted into her chamber. The familiar receding clatter died away, and she closed her eyes, too weary to think about rising to face another day of backbreaking work. There were crops to inspect, the garden needed tending, and today she must take a complete inventory of their dwindling supplies.

Fever had broken out among the slaves in several quarters, and their needs must be met as well. Although it seemed to be under control, the danger of a new outbreak was ever present. It was difficult to obtain the services of a doctor, so Kaitland had managed with home remedies and the few medical supplies her father had always kept on hand. The effectiveness of the Federal blockade was forcing the plantation owners to find all sorts of substitutes from natural sources. The woods had become a veritable drugstore. She had learned from Mrs. Pettibone that the value of the dogwood tree berries exceeded their beauty. They could be taken in place of quinine as they contained the alkaloid properties of cinchona and Peruvian bark. Blackberry roots and ripe persimmons were used for all manner of ailments including dysentery, and the list went on.

She smiled as she remembered the exact instructions of her knowledgeable neighbor. In the typical high-pitched whine, she spoke to Kaitland in her usual manner—as if she were still five years old.

In her half-dreamy state, she did not at first hear the sound of approaching horses. When the thundering beat of hooves grew close, her eyes flew open and she sprang from her bed, her heart racing wildly. Could it possibly be? She was almost afraid to look. There had been so many disappointments.

"Christopher." Her heart leaped simultaneously with a whispered gasp.

He rode into Glen More as she remembered him from that first morning many weeks ago. He was sitting relaxed and straight in the saddle with his bearing of confidence and pride.

Kaitland rushed around her room, frantically searching for the white dress she kept for special occasions. During the cool spring months, black was the color chosen for mourning, but white was acceptable during the hot, humid summer months. Out of respect for her father, she refrained from wearing colorful gowns.

She hurriedly pulled her hair back with two silver combs on either side, leaving it to flow its full length over her shoulders in thick waves. Many women wore hairpieces, but Kaitland had been blessed with an abundance of hair that could be arranged in many fashionable styles. Dulcie burst into the room out of breath from climbing the stairs too quickly.

"Miz Kaitlan', dat Yankee man is back again," she exclaimed, her black eyes with with apprehension. "What you s'pose he doin' comin' 'round here?"

"Dulcie, Lieutenant Donovan means us no harm. Now button my dress, please, and calm down." She gave away more of the excitement coursing through her quivering body than she intended. She was deliriously happy at the prospect of seeing Christopher again and wavered indecisively about changing into something more colorful.

Dulcie eyed her mistress with suspicion. "Miz Kaitlan', does I see a light in your eyes dat I ain't seen before? Chil', what is you thinkin'?"

The old Negro woman deftly buttoned Kaitland's dress of white, worked muslin. She straightened the graduated flounces over a fashionable hoop and fluffed the full-bell sleeves.

"Dat man ain't for you. Why he ain't nothin' but—"

"Dulcie! I'll not hear another word. All of us must follow our consciences, and Lieutenant Donavan is no exception. He has a job to do."

She whirled around to face the skeptical expression on Dulcie's plump face. It was impossible to deceive this crafty old woman. She could neither read nor write, but she possessed a keen perception of human nature.

Placing her hands on the slumped, aging shoulders of her friend, Kaitland smiled a bit guiltily. "Dulcie, you know me better than anyone now that Papa is gone. I don't know what I feel yet. I only know the prospect of seeing him again fills me with such excitement and joy. I've never felt this way before."

"Oh, honey chil', ol' Dulcie knows what you is feelin'. I jist don't want t' see you hurtin' no more. This man could bring real pain t' your young life. I been da onlyist ma you is had, an' you is like my very own. When you hurts, I hurts."

"I know and I appreciate your concern, but you're worrying needlessly. Now run along and ask Cook to prepare a hearty breakfast with coffee." Kaitland turned toward the mirror and smoothed the gathers around her tiny waist, arranging the full folds of her skirt.

"Miz Kaitlan', you know—"

"Yes, Dulcie, I know. There is less than half a tin of coffee left, but this is a special occasion. Now scoot!" She would make this breakfast as enjoyable as possible for Christopher.

She barely heard the servant's heavy sigh and grumblings as she closed the door.

Kaitland stood at the top of the stairs leaning against the balustrade. She watched tiny particles of dust dancing in the sunbeams that filtered through the tall, narrow louvered shutters on either side of the massive walnut door. The many-prismed crystal chandelier glistened and glinted, sending a rainbow of colors bouncing off the walls and

ceiling. She waited for the thud of his boots on the porch
and an impatient knock. Would he be impatient? After
these long weeks of no communication, would he be as
anxious to see her as she was to see him?

Suddenly she was jolted by the disturbing thought that
perhaps this time apart had dimmed his memory of her.
Perhaps the separation had—

Kaitland was startled from her reverie as a heavy foot-
fall scraped across the wide porch. The usual quick, determined stride was absent. There was a long pause. Was
it indecision, preparation, or was he attempting to control
the same flurry of emotions that coursed through her at
this moment? The strong feelings she held for this man
confused her, yet she could no longer deny the consuming
power he held over her.

Loud rapping from the brass door knocker reverberated
and echoed through the house, shattering the early morning peace and quiet. Kaitland descended from the shadows of the darkened hall, the fullness of her skirt rustling
with the movement. Dulcie approached, but Kaitland
waved her away. She wanted to greet Christopher alone.

"I'll answer the door, Dulcie. Please see to breakfast."

"Humph!" The old woman rolled her eyes and retreated
into the dining room.

When Kaitland opened the door, the hot odor of lathered
horses and sweating men permeated the morning air. She
was so stunned by the sight of Christopher she was unable
to speak. Her constricted throat caught in a silent gasp.
He was barely recognizable. Anger and resentment charged
through her for whatever circumstances had left him in
this condition.

He had lost weight, and his mud-encrusted uniform, a full size too large, hung loosely on his tall, lean frame. Dried rings of perspiration stained and further discolored the faded blue blouse. A full, black beard had replaced the usual clean-shaven face, and his hair had grown long with curling tufts hanging below his collar. The eyes, though tired and red-rimmed, were the same. She would know those expressive eyes anywhere. His gaunt, fatigue-lined features stirred such yearning and love within her. She wanted to hold him and make all the pain and misery go away. Seeing him again confirmed the one emotion she had refused to acknowledge. The pain of truth. She loved him.

"Christopher," was all she managed to whisper breathlessly, her eyes wide with concern. Did her face reveal what she had only moments ago admitted to herself?

"Kait . . . I . . . you are every bit as lovely as I remembered." He took a halting step forward. "You have filled my mind every day. I carried every memory with me, every detail of how you look, the sparkle in those eyes that can flash with fire one minute and love the next. Sometimes I could even smell the faint fragrance of lavender that spirals around you. A sunset reminded me of the way the light shines and shimmers on your hair—"

Lifting a hand, he lightly brushed her cheek, his thumb touching the faint darkening beneath her eyes. "Even now, I'm afraid if I blink just once you might disappear as the visions I held of you vanished during these weeks away from you."

Kaitland stood there silently hanging on to every word. He seemed so vulnerable, as if desperately reaching out to her for a lifeline. The intensity of the moment filled his features and his voice with heavy emotion, yet he barely spoke above a whisper.

Suddenly he stepped back, smiling apologetically. "Forgive me, Kait. My appearance must be offensive, but I am on a reconnaissance mission that brought me near Glen More. I took the opportunity to see you. There hasn't been much time for the basic necessities. It's been . . . so long. These weeks have seemed interminable, not knowing if I would ever see you again."

Their awareness of each other intensified as if they were trying to bridge the time apart.

"I know, for me as well. We've had only a few hours together, and so much left to say."

"How have you been, Kait?" *I've missed you,* her eyes told him.

"I'm well."

She suddenly felt the questioning stare of Christopher's men. Her slender body tensed, her cheeks growing hot with embarrassment. Although the men could not hear the conversation, it was not likely they missed the poignancy of the moment.

He must have sensed the reason for her discomfort and stepped between her and his inquisitive men. "I'm sorry, Kait. The men are tired and hungry." He rubbed his eyes as if to relieve and banish his own fatigue. "We've been in the saddle for days with only a few hours rest."

"Oh, Christopher, it is I who should apologize. I've kept you standing here when I should have asked you in. Please tell your men they may use the barn to rest. I'll send Amos with hot food and water for them. I'm having breakfast prepared for us, but I'm sure you will want to freshen up first."

He smiled and shook his head. "Who would ever suspect a lady of such femininity and domesticity could ride as well as most men and slip stealthily through enemy lines with the best of spies?" Lifting her hand, he kissed the sensitive palm, his eyes never leaving hers.

Kaitland was stunned by his reference to her spying. It was not a topic she wanted to discuss with him now. She hoped he did not intend to bring them back to the same debate. It had led to an impasse then, and it would surely evoke the same results now. They had so little time together and she did not want to spend it this way.

"Christopher, I don't—"

"Later, my love."

He gave his men the necessary orders and entered the foyer in time to hear Kaitland giving instructions to Amos.

"Amos, take Lieutenant Donovan to Papa's room and help him with a bath and anything else he requires."

"Da mas'r's room?! But, Miz Kaitland—"

"Yes, Amos, Papa's room." She imagined the disapproving thoughts running through the old man's mind, but it did not alter her decision.

"Yes, 'um, I do it, but I ain't gonna like it." Amos turned toward the stairs. "No, sir, I ain't gonna like it atall. Dat chil' is taken leave o' her senses."

Kaitland sensed Christopher's presence and turned, dropping her glance to her folded hands. "I'm sorry you heard that. It's just that he—"

"It's all right, love. I understand. He was devoted to your father, and I represent everything your father was against. I can have nothing but respect for such loyalty."

Scratching his bristly beard, Christopher started up the stairs. "Now let's see if I can separate myself from this bush I've grown accustomed to." He chuckled. "I hope Amos doesn't offer to shave me. He may decide a dead Yankee is the best kind."

"Please don't say such th—Christopher! You're not a lieutenant any longer. I just noticed the insignia on your uniform. Why it's captain now," she said, smiling. "You must be very proud."

"Field promotions are quite common. It's really not remarkable and simply means more responsibility." He half-turned and raised his brows questioningly. "Kait, are you still involved—"

"No questions, Christopher. As you said, we'll talk later, after you've eaten and rested." She avoided his eyes and moved away hurriedly to find Dulcie.

The sound of her small steps faded as she disappeared from view. "Kait, my love, can we ever have a future when we are not politically divided?" He sighed wearily, climbing the stairs.

&

The nagging question was sheer conjecture at this point and not based on fact. He had no way of knowing if she had stopped her covert activities. He doubted, however, a woman like Kaitland Trevilian would be easily swayed from fulfilling a commitment once made to herself and her cause. There had to be a way to work this out. He could no longer imagine life without her.

&

"That was the most delicious breakfast I've had in months."

Christopher patted his stomach and inhaled deeply of the
unusually cool July morning air. "Thanks for sharing your
coffee with me."

"I'm glad you enjoyed it. I save it for special occasions,
and I can't think of a more perfect time than this to appreciate one of our last remaining luxuries."

Her hand was tucked in the crook of his bent arm as they
walked among the trees near the house. Their steps were
muted, nearly imperceptible on the soft grass. Kaitland's
face was shaded by a large straw lavinia hat that tied under her chin. The fragrance of summer flowers hung heavy
in the air, filling their senses. Birds sang carefree melo-
dies, their symphony far removed from the screams of war.

"Did you find everything you needed in Papa's room?"
she asked anxiously. "I hope Amos didn't cause a problem."

His head tipped back, and he laughed heartily. "I think
I may have won your man over. Oh, he was a bit hostile at
first, but I drew him into a conversation and we parted—"

"Friends?" she asked hopefully.

"Well, I wouldn't go quite that far, but perhaps . . . in
time. He managed to clean and repair this uniform. It was
a remarkable feat considering the condition it was in. Perhaps his extra efforts on my behalf are a good sign."

"You look so much better. I was really very concerned
when I first saw you this morning."

"I know and I'm sorry, but a bath and shave, not to men-
tion a good meal, does wonders for a man. I couldn't come
this close to Glen More and not see you." His white teeth
flashed in a rakish grin.

Despite Christopher's improved appearance and glib

tongue, he was still drawn and thin. Recent weeks had not
been kind to him. At least he was alive and for that she
was thankful. She stopped and turned to face him.

"Christopher, is it very bad? The fighting I mean." With
quaking heart, she tried to imagine the dreadful experi-
ences he must have had and was certain her images were
far from the realities.

He half-turned to stare into the distance. His brow
creased and his features clouded as if remembering scenes
best forgotten. A myriad of emotions flitted across his
face, and it was several seconds before he answered. His
words were distant, as if he had been transported into the
past. The low timbre of his voice was a bit frightening,
almost menacing.

"I was caught in the middle of McClellan's continual
push despite deplorable weather and the relentless epidemics
of dysentery and recurring typhomalarial fever. Sense-
less, meaningless death and destruction. Men screaming
for help that never comes, the stench of dead animals;
manure; dead, mutilated men; and the acrid odor of gun-
powder burning your eyes and nostrils until you almost
wish for your own death to escape. Too little sleep and
poor rations for hungry men. Waves of humanity pitted
against each other, all positive of their own invincibility
and victory. When I close my eyes, I see the blood of the
wounded and dying. I relive the weeks of constant advances, retreats, and skirmishes. What has happened to
reason and rational, thinking men? The futility of this—"

Christopher blinked his watery eyes several times and
held his fist against them. His rigid body gradually relaxed, and he returned to the present.

"Forgive me, Kait. I didn't mean to become so carried away. It's just—"

She put her hands on his chest and peered into the dark depths of his eyes. "I'm sorry I asked. I had no idea the pain it would cause."

Restraint at this moment was not his strong point, and he suddenly enveloped her in a vicelike embrace. She slipped her arms around his thin body and held him, her head tucked into the curve of his neck. Neither spoke for several minutes. Words were unnecessary.

"Kait, I had to see you, to be certain you were all right. I know there has been fighting very close to Glen More. Have you been frightened?"

He leaned back, but kept her in the circle of his arms.

She chewed her lip, realizing where this conversation would lead. He would ultimately ask again about her undercover activities. Perhaps she could avoid that subject if she told him of the endless array of people who traveled to the plantation for assistance. Her confidence rallied as their eyes met, and she realized the extent of his concern.

"There were times when I felt afraid, but I've been too busy to dwell on it for long. There have been so many soldiers in need of help, and with the increasing difficulties of running this place, I—"

A sharp intake of breath and strangled sound from his throat stopped her in midsentence.

"Kaitland, have you taken in wounded men and tended them?"

She was perplexed by his outburst. What had she said? "Well . . . yes, but—"

Christopher dropped his arms and began pacing, anger

and frustration evident in his manner. With one swift movement, he placed his roughened tanned hand on the back of
his neck and rubbed it with an irregular motion. He stopped
abruptly and gripped her upper arms with such strength
she winced.

"For goodness sake, Kait, don't you realize the danger
of such actions. You are virtually alone here with a few
black servants. Taking in these men is asking for trouble.
When I think of what could have happened—"

"Please, Christopher, you're hurting me," she said, tears
gathering in her eyes.

His hands stopped their punishment and he folded her
gently in his arms. "I'm sorry, my sweet, trusting, naive
darling, but haven't you heard of what can . . . of the terrible things that . . ."

She smiled to herself and stepped back from his embrace. Poor dear. He was trying so hard to warn her
without actually saying the words. Her little contrivance
had only touched another one of his anxieties.

"Yes, I've heard, but nothing has happened. Those poor
men desperately needed help. One young boy died in my
arms. How could I have turned my back on him? He was
just a child," she said, her hands outstretched in a solicit-
ing gesture. "Things are not always black or white. Sometimes there are shadings that we must face with reality."

"Oh, Kait." He sighed heavily, turning away from her
in defeat. "You can be the most exasperating woman."
Running his fingers through the thickness of his hair, he
turned back, scowling darkly. "I hope you never see the
realities of this war," he murmured. "I don't want to see
you hurt or . . . worse. Please promise me you won't take

in any more wounded or any other strangers."

"I can't make a promise like that. I simply cannot turn a blind eye to those who come to me for help. Please try to understand."

"What you mean is, you won't. No, I don't understand. Forever the Good Samaritan, huh?"

The sarcastic remark and jeering glare cut her to the quick. A response froze in her throat.

"Kait, I'm only trying to protect you."

She had hoped for some remorse, but there was none. She was hurt, and anger reared its ugly head. The perfect day and the few precious moments with him were spoiled by his pigheadedness.

"I don't need your protection. Amos is always here, and I'm not afraid," she said, projecting more confidence than she felt.

"Amos! An old Negro and a handful of faithful slaves. How long do you think they could hold out against a determined group of hotheaded, self-seeking renegade soldiers?"

"Stop it, Christopher. You're being unreasonable and cruel." Burning tears sprang to her eyes, and she began to tremble with fury as she breathed in a choked sob.

"You can't begin to know the meaning of the word _cruelty_. You'll experience real cruelty if the wrong officer arrests you for spying."

"I'm very careful and—" She caught herself, but it was too late. Her brows came together sharply, and she stared at him with helpless regard. He had trapped her into saying just enough.

"So, you have continued to place yourself in jeopardy for a lost cause," he said in a resigned whisper. There was a hard-bitten set to his features and a wintry-dark frost to his gaze.

"Lost cause! Christopher, you—"

He pivoted and stalked away with angry, determined strides toward the barn. Over his shoulder he said, the harshness in his voice splintering the morning calm, "I don't want to hear it, Kait. I don't want to know anything about your Confederate loyalty. That little slip would cost your freedom if I followed military procedure instead of my heart. The less I know the clearer my conscience will be."

He stopped once, making a courtly bow as he said mockingly, "Thank you, madam, for your hospitality. I'm certain we shall meet again."

With that, he was gone without another word or a backward glance.

"Christopher, wait!" Anguished tears blurred her last glimpse of him, but his words were indelibly burned into her mind.

eight

Kaitland sat on a chaise absently toying with a leaf from an English ivy vine climbing the wide trellis of the porch. It had been four weeks since Christopher had left Glen More, and she had not heard from him. With each passing day, her behavior became more contrary and foreign to her true nature. She vacillated between depression and irascible mood swings that grew steadily worse. She had tried to chain her temper, but she could not seem to help herself.

The peninsula campaign was over, and the intense fighting had moved farther away from her land. She should be happy instead of moping about as though the entire war effort had been lost.

She wasn't happy, and the war had nothing to do with it. She had noticed faint circles under her large eyes growing darker. Cook had made every effort to prepare attractive meals, but the food had no taste at all. The poor darky just shook her head and clucked her tongue in disgust.

Christopher occupied her every waking thought, which was almost constant, for there were many sleepless nights. He had injured her pride and had mocked her faith, but worst of all, he had left without mending the breach between them. He expected too much of her. He wanted her to give up aiding the Confederacy while he continued to fight for the Union. *Well, I'll not do it*, she thought defiantly. *Neither will I turn away anyone who asks for help.*

If he had only said more before getting so angry. If he had only—

"Miz Kaitlan', is you goin' t' dat big ball in Richmond?"

"Oh, Dulcie, I didn't see you. The ball?" she said indifferently. "I really don't feel inclined to join in such festivities. Perhaps another time."

She hoped the noncommittal statement would dismiss the subject. The invitation from President Davis' staff to attend a fund-raising gala was open to all and did not require an answer. the taciturn mood that held her in its grip did not show any signs of leaving. A ball was the last thing on her mind.

"But, Miz Kaitlan', you needs t' get out more. You cain't jist sit 'round here amoonin' after dat Yankee."

"That will do, Dulcie," she snapped. "I'm not mooning, as you put it. I have a great deal on my mind."

"Yes, 'um dats a fact, but dat ain't no call t' act this way." The old woman put up her hand to silence her mistress from responding.

"Now, chil', I ain't gonna shut my mouth 'til you has listen t' me good. I knows you love dat man, and I knows he loves you. Why, a body'd have t' be blind t' miss da eye-gogglin' he gives you, and dat boy done have his feelin's wrote all over dat handsome face. Now, I been watchin' you for weeks, and I knows what's robbin' you of your peace of mind. And don't tell me it's da war."

The rapidly fired observations of the maid and her determined stance showed her overindulgence with Kaitland's unsociable behavior was at an end.

"Oh, Dulcie, he couldn't love me and leave as he did without a word. He was so angry with me."

"Now, chil', dat be a man. When dey is fresh in love, dey acts all kinds o' ways and does crazy things too. Ol' Dulcie atellin' you da straight of it. Dat man'll be back wid hat'n hand," she said positively, a broad grin creasing her plump cheeks. "You jist leave da rest t' da Laud. Now dat ball be jist three days away, and dat'll jist 'bout be enough time t' get you all gussied up."

Kaitland thought for a while before responding. "You're right, Dulcie. Why should I allow myself to be miserable." Christopher probably had not given her a second thought since he left.

"Dat's my baby, and if I be knowin' anythin' 'bout menfolks, dat Yankee boy is ahurtin' jist like you is."

Kaitland doubted that, but she was not going to let it dampen her spirits now that she had decided to go. She stood up excitedly, then sobered and asked anxiously, almost as an afterthought. "He will be back, won't he, Dulcie?"

"Yes, 'um, dat he will, honey, dat he will."

Lucinda rattled on about first one thing then another as the carriage creaked and rumbled along the road near the outskirts of Richmond. Kaitland had consented to go to the ball with Lucinda Monroe and her father rather than attend alone. It would have been unwise to take Dulcie and Amos away for two days, leaving Glen More unattended.

"Aren't you excited, Kaitland? Why there will be scads of unattached men at the ball! Can't you just imagine how delightful that will be?"

"What? Oh yes, Lucinda, it should be great fun," she acknowledged disinterestedly. Try as she may, she was

finding it impossible to concentrate on anything except
Christopher. There was no getting away from the way she
felt about him. Perhaps she would receive an assignment
this evening. That would take her mind off him, for the
time being, and give her something else to think about.

"Kaitland, you haven't heard a word I've said."

Lucinda's pouting only served to raise Kaitland's hack-
les, but she quickly subdued an outburst. Lucinda was a
bit immature, but she meant well. Under ordinary circumstances, this evening would have filled her with excitement as well. "I'm sorry, Lucinda. I suppose I'm a little
preoccupied."

"What is wrong, Kaitland? We haven't seen each other
for weeks, and here is an opportunity for us to catch up
and you practically ignore me."

"Now, Lucy, honey. Kaitland has a lot of responsibility." Mr. Monroe spoke for the first time since leaving
Glen More. He had appeared to be asleep, but apparently
heard every word they had said.

"Well, Papa, it's true. I miss seeing her."

"Lucinda, please forgive me. I'll try to push everything
else from my mind and concentrate on the ball."

"Well, if you say so. Now, as I was saying . . ."

Kaitland's and Lucinda's wraps were taken by a servant
when they entered the elegant foyer of the Grover mansion. They were then ushered into a beautifully furnished
parlor where they were greeted by their host and hostess,
Mr. and Mrs. Mordecai Grover. Mrs. Grover politely
guided them through the receiving line where they were
presented to President and Mrs. Jefferson Davis and a number of his staff members.

Heads turned as admiring eyes lingered on Kaitland, attired in her ball dress of white Chambery gauze, immensely full and trimmed with white satin folds and blond lace. Full lace sleeves topped with pink satin bows, a pink rose centered on the narrow lace-edged neckline, created a striking beauty. It was set off by a wide, pink sash tied snugly around her tiny waist, flowing gracefully down the length of her gown. Her hair had been arranged in the fashionable waterfall style and adorned with small pink satin bows.

The natural flow of guests moved into an enormous salon where furniture and rugs had been removed except for chairs placed around the room to leave ample space for dancing. The dance had already begun, and ladies in their dazzling full gowns and men in their finest Confederate dress whirled about the dance floor to a Strauss tune.

Lucinda had been right about one thing: There certainly was an abundance of men who, Kaitland estimated, outnumbered the women five to one.

"Oh, Kaitland, isn't this just the most thrilling evening of your life?'" Lucinda bubbled with excitement, tapping her foot to the three-four time.

Before she could respond, Lucinda accepted a dance from a dashing lieutenant. Moments later, Kaitland found herself dancing with a young Confederate officer bent on fracturing each toe she possessed, one at a time. She was extremely grateful when he excused himself and approached Lucinda. Kaitland smothered a giggle when her friend's delighted smile turned to distress. The young man seemed oblivious to the physical pain he was inflicting.

"I promise to spare your feet if you'll honor me with a dance."

She spun around at the sound of the soft familiar voice. "Tim! How nice to see you."

"I've been waiting for you to arrive. I'd almost given up hope. Then the room suddenly began to sparkle, and I knew that you had arrived."

His gentle smile saddened her, knowing how he felt about her. "Tim Carrington, you're still full of the blarney," she said, laughing gaily.

"It's not blarney, Kait. You do sparkle, and your smile would light up any room." He took her hand, maneuvering her onto the dance floor as the musicians struck up the beginning strains of a waltz.

"How are things for you, Kait? I haven't seen you lately."

As was the custom in waltzing to a Strauss tune, the couples moved clockwise during the first half, then, when the refrain was about to be repeated, they stopped momentarily before resuming in a counterclockwise flow. Kaitland waited for the turn to be completed before answering.

"I miss Papa, but I manage quite well, actually. Glen More is holding its own, all things considered. The war has inflicted hardship on everyone," she said slowly. "We're probably better off than most landowners. We were fortunate to have reserve supplies of some basic necessities. I suppose we're learning just what constitutes those things we can't live without." She smiled. "It's a short list."

He stared over the top of her head, frowning as if perplexed. Something or someone was distracting his attention.

"Is something wrong, Tim?"

"Mmmm, oh no. I just thought I saw someone who looked familiar," he said a bit guardedly, then whirled her toward the punch table. He poured her a glass of punch and excused himself, saying he had seen an old friend and wanted to speak to him.

"Kaitland, will you honor an old man and have this waltz with me. I fear the next dance might be a polka or a schottische, and these tired old bones aren't up to that."

"Of course, Mr. Monroe."

She stared at Tim's retreating back, but there was no time to dwell on his strange behavior.

Offering his arm to Kaitland, the portly gentleman swept them away, amazingly light on his feet and in perfect step with the music.

"How have you been, my dear? Keeping up with the rigors of plantation management, are you?" he asked, puffing from the exertion. "My daughter dominated the conversation on our journey this evening, and I didn't have a chance to inquire."

"Yes, thank you. As well as anyone these days."

"Good, good. I should have offered more assistance, but with my own place and Mrs. Monroe's illness, I—"

"It's quite all right, Mr. Monroe. I understand."

She had the distinct impression he had been hoping for more detailed answers. She had always wondered if perhaps he suspected her activities went beyond the care of Glen More. He had never asked about Christopher's visit the day after her father's death, but she knew his interest went further than simple curiosity. It was best if no one knew what she was doing, except Amos. Mr. Monroe would not have approved. His opinion was that a woman's place should be restricted to the home, to the care and feeding of the lord and master.

The dance ended, and she thought he meant to say more, but he excused himself and headed for the punch bowl, dabbing his brow.

As she turned to find a chair, her eyes fell on a strikingly handsome Confederate major whose dark eyes were boring into her. He was wearing a perfectly fitted officer's uniform with its short jacket, its braid decorations on the sleeves, stand-up collar, cuffs and trouser stripes of infantry blue. His trim waist was cinched with a black-webbed belt and clip.

Suddenly, she felt the blood draining from her head. She felt faint, and stifled a gasp, her eyes widened with shock. She tried to take a deep breath against the gathering tightness in her chest, but her lungs seemed paralyzed, unable to function.

Christopher was instantly by her side lending support, so naturally, the incident failed to attract the attention she might have expected.

The band was beginning another waltz, and Christopher seized the opportunity to further support her by spinning her away among the other couples. Neither had spoken, and he watched her with an intense gaze that came to rest on the gentle curve of her mouth. Did he realize, she wondered, how overpowering the aura of his masculinity was or of the strength and determination he exuded?

"Feeling better?" he asked in that deep disturbing voice, each syllable caressing her. He held her gently, yet the latent power of his strength was unmistakable, poised and ready for action.

"What are you doing here?" she finally asked, finding her voice.

"Smile, darling. Everyone will think we are quarreling," he whispered close to her ear, sending a shiver over her heated body.

"May I say there are none so lovely in all of Richmond as you." The compliment was uttered loud enough for the benefit of those couples who were dancing close by. It was imperative they avoid attracting attention to themselves. His life could well depend on his remaining incognito.

"Christopher, please. Why are you dressed in a—oh no," she groaned, closing her eyes in disbelief.

"Yes, my sweet. Quite a turn of events, wouldn't you say?"

She leaned into his hard body, violating the proper distance between two dancers who were supposedly strangers. They skirted the other dancers, moving toward long windows that opened onto the terrace. The cool, early fall air clashed with Kaitland's flushed skin, immediately reviving her. The scent of late-blooming flowers from the garden mingled with the pungent odor of the cigar-smoking gentleman who had retreated to smoke near the garden wall.

Christopher led her to a darkened area of the terrace that would afford them privacy.

"Before you say anything, Kait, I want to apologize for my behavior when we last met. It was inexcusable, and I'm deeply sorry for leaving in such an angry state. I had no right to question you. You have a kind heart, and I was wrong in my assessment of the situation. That doesn't mean I don't worry about you, but after thinking more clearly later, I realized the predicament you were in. I've been miserable every day and night since. Will you forgive me?" He took her hands in his and kissed each palm, his lips lingering on their softness.

The sincerity of his words brought tears to her eyes and joy to her burdened heart. He had been thinking about her during these long weeks and had been as miserable as she.

"Of course I forgive you. I, too, have been in a terrible state. Everyone at home will attest to that." She smiled, thinking about Dulcie's lecture. "I'm so sorry for my harsh words. We were both upset," she whispered regretfully. "I see now that you were only concerned about my safety. And you were right about taking in strangers. It is a very dangerous practice."

"I wrote to you several times, but never sent the letters. I couldn't find adequate words to express how I felt. When I heard of this assignment I volunteered, hoping you would be in attendance."

She stepped back and looked up into his undisguised features. She thought she would always remember him this way with the evening breeze ruffling his dark hair. Her mind suddenly assailed her with reality and the reason for his being here, but none of them mattered now. All of their time together had been stolen minutes filled with secret glances. It would always be so as long as they were on opposing sides in this dreadful war.

"Christopher, you're here as a spy, aren't you?" she whispered painfully.

He smiled boyishly, an expressive lift to his wide shoulders admitting his deception. "It would seem so, my love. Ironic isn't it? Two spies, standing face-to-face, having vowed loyalty to their respective causes. Perhaps it would be prudent now to ask the question you once put to me. Are you going to have me arrested?"

"If you thought I might have you arrested, why did you come?" She looked into his intent features. He was so honest and straightforward, and he trusted her. Each could have had the other arrested at some point during their acquaintance, but neither one was able to do it.

"Do you always answer a question with a question?" he said, smiling down at her. "It . . . seemed worth the risk." His voice lay gently on the star-studded night air while his dark gaze captured and held her like a serpent mesmerized and held its prey. His warm lips brushed a light kiss on her temple, then her cheek where his mouth lingered for a moment before pulling her into his embrace, their shadows merging as one.

The emotional flood that was building inside her felt as though it would burst, drawing her into a swirling maelstrom of no return, to a place of shadows and pain, of pleasure and joy. She responded by sliding her arms around him, her fingers intertwining behind his neck. Her breath caught in her throat and a tremor of expectancy raced through her trembling body. He groaned, his hard lips finding hers with such thoroughness and intensity it shook the very foundation of her being.

"Kait, Kait," he murmured huskily against her lips, his warm breath labored. "I wish I were free to tell you . . . but this war . . . I—"

She swayed a bit when Christopher moved away and stepped to the terrace railing, his strong support removed. A shadow darkened his gaze for an instant, and she sensed a change in the heightened atmosphere around them.

"Christopher, we haven't much time. I'll be missed. Please finish what you started to say. Heaven only knows when we will see each other again." She desperately needed to know if he felt the same as she did. There was so much that should be said and so little time in which to say it.

"Don't you mean if we see each other again?"

Kaitland's sharp intake of breath nearly choked her. "Christopher, don't think that way," she whispered fervently. So that was it. "The war can't last forever. I know we're involved in dangerous work, but—"

"Dangerous! This mission I'm on right now has brought this entire mess into perspective. If ever I had any doubts about the jeopardy in which you place yourself, I certainly have none now. I—" He faltered, his voice growing hoarse, his dark eyes glittering in the moonlight. "Oh, Kait, don't you see? Our future is so uncertain. It wouldn't be fair to make commitments." The frustration and hopelessness in his tone was enough to silence her.

She said no more, for it was, after all, the man's place to pursue a relationship. It seemed so unfair. Didn't her feelings count? Calming her raw nerves was impossible. She felt unsure of herself in the wake of Christopher's indecision. The despair she was experiencing was stifling.

"Do you understand why I have to do . . . what I do?" She must know if he had come to terms with her commitment to the cause.

He turned, moving to stand in front of her. His eyes flashed, but his voice was subdued. "I'm trying, Kait. I'm sincerely making an effort to understand what drives and motivates you. This faith you speak of must really work, at least for you. Although I realize the work you do goes beyond that. We've been over this before, I know, but it's all so complicated. Perhaps one day we'll look back and it will seem so simple."

His words revealed a sense of astonishment without a hint of mockery, and they were more accepting than before. Lifting his head, a sigh shuddered through him. Pressing a kiss between her brows and brushing her eyelids, he cupped her cheek with his raised hand. His thumb smoothed the gentle shape of her mouth. "You are so lovely."

The beginning strains of a polonnaise drifted through the open windows. They stood facing each other, drinking in, committing to memory every feature, every line and play of emotion mirrored in their faces. The few seconds remaining to them must become part of their total beings. The future was indeed uncertain.

"Kait, I—"

"Ah, there you are, Kaitland. I believe this dance is mine."

Tim offered her his arm, and she gave a reluctant gesture of assent. The interruption startled her, plunging her back into the world of realities and pain, of separation and death. Her mind was slow to respond, but the intrusion was demanding and insistent.

Tim bowed stiffly in Christopher's direction, smiling with satisfaction. Whisking Kaitland away, he left Christopher alone in the shadows. She glanced over her shoulder and saw his raised hand in a gesture of irritation. It would be fatal for him if she acknowledged anything other than casual conversation with him. A pang of regret shot through her, and she lowered her lashes against the softness of her cheeks to conceal the longing she knew was revealed in her eyes.

The polonnaise was a triple-time Polish dance, allowing little conversation between dance partners. The music came to an abrupt stop, leaving Kaitland breathless. She readily accepted the offer of a glass of punch.

Christopher had been watching the couple from the doorway, his expressionless face revealing nothing. When the dance was concluded, he casually ambled to the punch table and proceeded to introduce himself to Tim.

Kaitland's heart lurched as she stiffened, her grasp on

the punch glass tightening instinctively. What was he doing? This was an insane game he was playing.

"Excuse me, Captain. I don't believe we've met. I'm Major Creighton Darlington of the First Maryland Regiment." Christopher extended his hand to the younger officer who responded in an acceptable manner, but his impassive face betrayed the reservation. Only a slight narrowing of his eyes and a barely perceptible tensing of his body bore evidence of the disquiet building inside him.

She couldn't believe what was happening. What did Christopher hope to gain?

"Captain Timothy Carrington, First Virginia Infantry, at your service, sir."

Kaitland stared at the two men quizzically, holding her breath. Why was Tim being so reserved? It wasn't like him. Was it because he had found her with Christopher on the darkened terrace?

"You must have been with Jackson in the Shenandoah Valley, Major. He's a great General."

Tim's statement revealed his natural interest in the war, but Kaitland was reacting to strange signals. Something was wrong. She had known Tim all her life, and his manner was anything but natural or even cordial.

"He's brilliant, Captain, simply brilliant. A pleasure to have served with him. You've seen some major victories on the peninsula yourself. You certainly drove McClellan into the sea," Christopher said, pouring a second glass of punch.

Kaitland listened in amazement. She was becoming more confused and nervous with the passing of every second.

"Yes, well, we suffered badly in several battles; the outcome, however, has been most rewarding, Major," Tim said cautiously, sipping the tart liquid.

Turning to Kaitland, his blue eyes searching her face, Tim asked, "How long have you known the Major, Kait?"

Her glance at Christopher's impassivity gave her no hint as to how she should respond. "Why . . . uh, we only met this evening," she said softly.

"Oh? When I came looking for you, it appeared to be an acquaintance of much longer standing."

"Captain, I must apologize for monopolizing Miss Trevilian's time and the seemingly questionable circumstances under which you found us on the terrace, but I can assure you the lady and I only just met. We went to the terrace for a breath of fresh air, and I'm afraid I got carried away relating the intricacies of major battles while under General Jackson's command."

Christopher's relaxed explanation was perfect as he easily extricated them from a potentially explosive situation.

"Of course, Major. My apologies for jumping to conclusions," Tim said, his lips parting slightly with a smile that didn't quite reach his eyes.

"Accepted, Captain."

The two men bowed stiffly, bringing their glasses together in a mock toast, each still wary of the other. Kaitland sensed a silent duel being waged between them as each carefully measured the other.

Christopher had not given her the name he was using so it had been impossible for her to introduce them. He had placed himself in further jeopardy by striking up this conversation with Tim in order to protect her. If Tim had asked her the Major's name, she seriously doubted he would have accepted her ignorance of it. He had known her too long to believe she would be alone with a man whose name she did not know.

"Tell me, Captain, did you see the ironclad *Monitor* on the James River at Fort Darling?"

Christopher stopped in midsentence, but it was too late. He had carelessly used the Union name of Fort Darling for the Confederate stronghold, Drewry's Bluff. No loyal Confederate officer would have made such a blunder. He had unwittingly exposed his identity as a spy.

Kaitland heard Tim's swift indrawn breath as his sharp, blue eyes cut into Christopher's. Her startled gaze met his glance briefly, then flicked away, dreading the next few moments. The air became charged, both men standing motionless and tense, preparing for the inevitable. Their eyes locked, each realizing the deadly slip of the tongue.

She cleared her dry throat and placed a hand on Tim's arm. "Tim, please. Perhaps—"

"Stand aside, Kaitland," he said tersely, never taking his piercing eyes from Christopher. "I made a few discreet inquiries about the good Major. No one seems to know him. Now I understand why.

"Major, you can come quietly without causing a scene, or I can arrest you here and disrupt the festivities, frightening the good ladies of Richmond. The choice is yours." Tim spoke in low menacing tones, and there was no mistaking the underlying meaning. He would do whatever was necessary to see Christopher behind bars or hanged.

"I suppose you have me, Captain. There is no need to disturb this lovely affair. I will come peacefully."

Before turning toward the entrance hall where all sidearms had been left by soldiers in attendance, he glanced at Kaitland. With infinite care he raised her hand to his lips, brushing over the sensitive skin. His fathomless, dark eyes searched her face as if to draw part of her into himself. "Until we meet again, my sweet," he whispered for her ears alone.

The two men strode casually through the crowd and left the room. Kaitland followed in their shadows, struggling desperately to conceal the intense emotions coursing through every nerve in her body. Tim immediately extracted the nearest pistol from its holster and thrust the barrel against Christopher's back. They left the house and were swallowed up in the darkness of the city street, moving toward the Confederate headquarters two blocks away. The streets were nearly deserted, but no one would have found it unusual for soldiers to be strolling with a lady in the Confederate Capitol. Apparently their departure was unnoticed by anyone at the dance, since couples were coming and going throughout the evening.

"Kaitland, I think it would be best if you returned to the dance," Tim said in a flat, professional manner. He had stopped between two gas lamps on the street, their faces bathed in a soft glow.

She faced him in the semidarkness, glancing uncertainly toward Christopher. She could make out his profile, then he turned his head and winked at her, nodding slightly. Was it a signal? Her instincts told her it was. She must help him.

"Tim, are you really arresting this man?"

"Of course," he said as he watched Christopher. "He's a spy. What would you have me do?"

She must gain his attention and give Christopher the few seconds he needed. It would be dangerous, but peril was a daily companion for all of them. He would have known the risks when he signaled her. She was certain a hazardous escape was preferable to prison for him. Her heart pounded against her chest as numbness gripped her, the muscles in her legs beginning to quiver. The life of the man she loved was in her hands.

Kaitland furtively slipped a foot from her black kid slipper and turned to take a step. She deliverately stumbled into Tim, knocking the gun away from Christopher's back.

"Oh, my shoe."

Tim grunted from the sudden unexpected jolt, catching her but thrown off balance. His recovery was further hindered by Kaitland's full hoopskirt that billowed about their feet. As she had planned, it was long enough for Christopher to lunge forward, break into a lope, and disappear into the darkness.

Tim steadied her and raised his pistol, taking aim at the fading image just beyond the streetlamp on the corner of the block.

"No," Kaitland screamed, grabbing Tim's arm causing the shot to go wild.

He turned on her with fury flashing in his eyes, his breathing heavy and agitated. She had never seen his face so dark with anger.

"What the—Kaitland, why did you do that? He got away!" he fumed.

Warm tears spilled from her eyes. Her audible sob was the only sound on the street except for a barking dog and the distant rattle of a carriage on the cobblestones.

Tim relented and gathered her trembling body close to him. "Oh, Kait. You've known him for months, haven't you? You wouldn't have protected a Union spy unless he meant something to you. I should have seen it. I'm beginning to understand a lot of things now.

"He's the one, isn't he? He's the man I've lost out to," he said defeatedly. "Why did it have to be a Yankee, of all people?"

She looked up, the tears streaming unchecked down her pale cheeks. She dabbed her eyes with a handkerchief offered by Tim. It took her a few minutes to compose herself before she answered. It pained her to see the hurt and defeat in Tim's face, but she could not hide her relationship with Christopher any longer.

"Tim, I would give anything to have spared you this. Please don't be angry. I had no idea Christopher would be here. He had volunteered, hoping to see me and—" Fresh tears filled the emerald-green beauty of her eyes, choking off further words.

"It's all right. I'm not angry. I see things clearly now. It just cuts deep to have lost your affections to a Yankee." He smiled slowly, returning to the quick and easy good humor so characteristic of Tim, despite his bitter disappointment.

"Christopher, huh? Nice name. Now, let's see one of those dazzling smiles that has sent every young man at the ball begging for just one dance."

"Oh, Tim, I don't deserve a friend like you. Thank you," she cried, making a feeble effort to smile. "He will be all right, won't he?" Sudden anxiety invaded her features.

"Well, you surely saw to that, my dear. Yes, I'm sure he got away. He has a good head start on any search party."

"Search!" Kaitland's eyes widened with alarm.

Hurried footsteps were descending upon them. Several uniformed men who had been at the ball ran toward them with drawn pistols.

"Let me handle this, Kait," Tim whispered in her ear.

"What's going on here, Carrington? We heard a shot fired!" one man inquired, wielding his handgun excitedly.

"Yeah. Are you all right?" asked another.

The men eyed Kaitland, bewildered but saying nothing.

"A spy, gentlemen. I discovered him impersonating a Confederate officer and arrested him quietly. I saw no need to disrupt the dance. When we reached this darkened area, he made a run for it." Tim gestured in the opposite direction from the place where Christopher had disappeared.

"I fired but missed. Perhaps you could organize a search party while I take Miss Trevilian back to Mrs. Grover. This entire episode has upset her terribly."

Before they could respond or inquire as to Kaitland's presence during an arrest, he rushed her away from the dumbfounded men.

"I'll take you back to the house then join the search. Perhaps I can make certain your young man isn't discovered."

"How can I ever thank you, Tim?"

"Don't ask me to dance at your wedding," he said flashing a broad teasing smile.

nine

Kaitland slipped to the back of the Grover house during the confusion sparked by Tim's gunshot. She felt it best to elude curious eyes and inevitable questions from the guests attending the ball. She made her way to her assigned room by using the stairway that led from the east garden to the second floor of the house. Out-of-town guests were often given overnight accommodations by the host since these affairs often lasted until the early morning hours.

The muted sounds of voices intermingled with the strains of the orchestra drifted through the open window. Meager light from the moon caught the ivory sheen of lace curtains as they billowed in the soft breeze.

Kaitland stood in the darkness trying to concentrate on controlling her labored breathing. The air was warm and humid, but she was cold and trembling. Chills of fear raised the hair on her arms and neck and a cold sweat prickled every inch of her body. She wrapped her arms around herself and sank to the floor, leaning against the bed. Gradually she began to relax. She had to calm herself down before she could think rationally.

Christopher had escaped. . .or had he? She had made it possible for him to run, but had the search party cornered him somewhere? Surely, he had planned for such a contingency. It would be madness to volunteer for a dangerous assignment and not weigh all possibilities carefully.

Of course his prime objective had been to see her rather than gather information that might be of help to the Union. That reason alone rendered him vulnerable if not careless.

What to do. Kaitland nibbled her bottom lip. He may have hidden in the immediate area. Perhaps she should look for him. But where?

Mrs. Grover had offered a housemaid to see to Kaitland's needs for the duration of her stay in Richmond. She would certainly be checking the room soon to turn down the bed and help her undress. The presence of a servant complicated things.

As she thought of Christopher, a smile played at the corners of her mouth. She opened her small travel trunk and pushed aside the silk and satin articles of clothing which lay on top. There on the bottom were the worn trousers, boots, shirt, and hat. She changed in record time then arranged the pillows under the coverlet in hopes it would resemble a sleeping form. If the maid came to the door and looked in she would assume that Kaitland had retired early because of her ordeal in the street and quietly leave reporting to Mrs. Grover that poor Kaitland was resting.

It was not exactly the proper thing to do, but she doubted anyone would question her actions. Tim would verify her state of mind after the incident. Lucinda was sure to be inquisitive, but she would deal with the little miss busybody in the morning.

Kaitland paused by the door listening for sounds on or around the darkened stairway. She cautiously made her way down the stairs and into the alleyway without intrusion. She moved through the shadows feeling rather proud of herself. She had become quite adept at eluding detection. If her plan worked, she would have the rest of the night to look for Christopher.

ѧ

Christopher lay in the hay loft brushing aside wisps of straw that tickled his face and neck. He had stumbled onto a livery stable after dashing down a side street barely three blocks from the Grover mansion. He had heard hurried footsteps just ahead and darted into the stable seeking refuge in the loft. He did not have the advantage of the search party who knew the intricate turning of every street and alley. His meager knowledge was limited to his one trip to Richmond that evening dressed as a Confederate officer. He was hoping the Rebels would be more interested in the lure of the pretty ladies at the dance than a spy who had probably fled the area.

"Did you see anything, Randy?"

"Nah. That Yankee could be anywhere by now." The two men were directly below the loft where Christopher held his breath, willing himself to absolute stillness. He was weaponless and a scuffle with these men would surely alert the others.

"Aw, c'mon," one of the soldiers said, "let's go find the Captain and tell him he's gone. It's too dark anyway. He's probably back at the dance sniffin' around that redhead I saw him with in the garden. Officer or not, he's got things on his mind that ain't got nothin' to do with a spy." Both men laughed and left the barn.

Christopher breathed a sigh of relief. Now was his chance if he could find his way back to his horse. Darting down dark unfamiliar alleys had confused his sense of direction. As he stepped down from the last rung of the loft ladder, he heard a noise. Someone was opening the livery door. He froze, then edged to the wall near the entrance. Night had crept in with its stealthy cloak of darkness and he strained to see. A half-moon hung in the sky obscured by cloud cover.

A slight figure slipped through the door, then stopped. He seemed to sense Christopher's presence. As he started to turn, Christopher, like a striking viper, grabbed the intruder from behind clasping one arm around his middle while covering the man's mouth with his other hand. He was momentarily surprised at how slender the furiously kicking, struggling man was. He must have captured the stable boy and no doubt scared him half to death.

"Stop fighting me. I won't hurt you," Christopher whispered hoarsely. "Just be calm. I'll let you go, but you have to promise to be still." Christopher eased him to the floor and the boy relaxed. "Not a sound. Do I have your promise?" There was a slight nod in response. Christopher took a deep breath and groaned. "Oh no." He released Kaitland and turned her so that she was facing him. "Kait. What are you doing here?" he rasped.

"Is this the way you repay someone who helped you escape? How did you know it was me? You can't see a thing in here."

He could hear the smile in her voice as he lifted her off the ground wrapping her in a bear hug. "You crazy woman. Stable boys don't wear lavender."

"Oh. A small infraction. I hadn't planned to travel in buckskins tonight," she said soberly, contemplating her outfit.

"How on earth did you find me?"

"You forget what I do under the cover of darkness," she said.

"No, I haven't forgotten."

It hurt her to hear the grave quality of his voice, but she forced herself to ignore it. "Are you all right?" she asked anxiously.

"Yes, but neither of us will be if we don't figure how to get out of here." He tried to see her face in the black shadows. He took her icy hands in his. "Your hands are cold," he whispered.

"And yours are warm," she murmured and went willingly into his arms that enveloped and held her. He was solid and powerful. His strong body became a momentary safe haven; a few seconds reprieve from whatever destiny awaited them. A wave of pure pleasure washed over her. The warmth she felt in Christopher's presence was no longer a mystery. While she had admitted to herself that she loved this very special man, she realized how little she knew about him.

Reluctantly, Christopher released her. "We have to get out of here, Kait. Someone could come in at any minute."

"I know." She drew a deep, steadying breath. His nearness tended to muddle the flow of the logic. "I think I know a safe place not far from here."

"Lead the way. I am completely at your mercy."

His attempt at levity was lost on Kaitland for she had assumed the alerted readiness that overtook her mind and body when vital caution was necessary to her safety.

They moved as one through the black night. Christopher marveled at Kaitland's agility and unwavering single-mindedness of mission. There was little wonder why the Confederacy valued her so highly. His assessment of her had been correct from the first day they met. She was quite a woman.

Kaitland took his hand in hers and with lithe, quick steps she led him to the rear entrance of a small shop. "Wait here. I'll light a lamp. There are no windows in here so we won't be discovered." The smell of sulfur and kerosene mingled with the damp, musty odor stinging their eyes and nostrils as the glowing flame illuminated the room. "It's a gunsmith shop. My cousin runs it. He's very careless about locking up. I used to come here with my father when I was a child. The place always fascinated me," she said, running a finger along the edge of a workbench in the center of the room.

Christopher looked around, obviously impressed with the array of weapons and various parts he saw neatly stored on the floor-to-ceiling shelves. "Guns intrigue you?" he asked.

"Not very ladylike is it?" Kait stared down at her folded hands.

"It make you no less a lady, Kait. That's something you couldn't change if you tried." He touched her cheek with the back of his fingers. "Kait, how can I ever thank you for what you did back there?"

"There's no need. You must know why I did it." She grasped his hand and held it.

"Ah, my lovely Kait. What am I going to do about you?"

Tell me you love me, she wanted to say, but knew she could not. If he ever said those words to her it would not be because she prompted him. A smile of regret touched her lips. "What do you want to do?" Apprehension knotted her stomach.

"It would seem that taking you into custody is out of

the question."

Kaitland saw the twinkle in his eye, his voice lacking conviction, but her temper suddenly flared. She stepped back and turned away from him. "Well why don't you just *do* it and salve your bluebelly conscience." Unable to stop the flow of words she spun around piercing him with a furious glare. Her eyes shooting green sparks, intense and stinging, she blurted, "Arrest me and have done with it." She regretted the words as soon as they had passed her lips, but didn't the man realize that every second counted? There was not time for unnecessary conversation.

A faint frown shadowed his eyes and he spread his hands in a resigned gesture. "Kait, please. I didn't mean that the way it sounded. You didn't let me finish. I could never arrest you now or ever and I'm certainly not in a position at the moment to do so. I told you that. We're in this together now, each protecting the other regardless of the ethics involved. Don't you see?"

She put her balled fists on her hips and glared at him. Striding toward her, he folded his hands around her upper arms. The emotion in his voice gave her pause. Words froze in her throat. She was being so unfair. Christopher had protected her from the beginning to the point of placing his own life in jeopardy. He was the quintessential soldier, but he had gone against everything he believed in for her sake. The dark brown gaze that met hers deepened slightly, intelligent and intense. A fission of awareness shuddered through her. Tears welled in her eyes but she blinked them away.

His lips twitched with a smile, then his deep, timbre laughter filled the room. "Tsk, tsk, such language, Miss Trevilian. Bluebelly indeed. Darling, you're in a category all by yourself." He gave her an easy smile. "It would be such a waste to put you behind bars. No, your arrest hasn't been on my agenda since the day I came to your room after your fall. If it had been we would not be having this conversation. You would be in jail."

"Now what, Christopher?" she questioned ruefully. Her anger had subsided as quickly as it had come.

After a moment's pause, he continued. "I know what I said on the terrace tonight. I still feel strongly about making commitments at this time, but I had a little time to think back there in the livery." He looked at the ridiculous hat that concealed Kaitland's hair and pushed it from her head. Her face was instantly framed with a riot of glorious shades of shimmering gold and red with streaks of cinnamon. He threaded his fingers through her tresses, gently tilting back her head so that he could better see her face. "A decided improvement," he said, smiling.

She looked straight into his eyes, his warm breath brushing her face. For a moment, a bemused expression touched his features, but was soon replaced with confidence, even determination.

"Kait, I've never met anyone like you. There is a depth of understanding, of honesty that flows so naturally with fluid grace in your every feature. You lead with your heart, my love, and you have become the most important thing in my life. I love you, and I'm asking you to wait for me until the war is over. Perhaps I don't have the right, but I'll take my chances."

With hot, dry tears burning her throat, her voice husky, she answered, "Yes, I'll wait for you." She clung to him with a hint of ferocious desperation, very much aware of the energy flowing between them.

"Are you sure, Kait? You answered rather quickly."

"It seems I've waited all my life to hear you say those words. I think I fell in love with you the minute our eyes met at Glen More, the day you came to search my house and grounds.

"Tell me it won't be much longer. Tell me that you see an end in sight to this war."

Her entreaty tore at his heart because he could not give her the assurance she wanted. "I wish with every fiber of my being that I could give you the answer you want to hear, but I can't. The fighting grows more intense and bloody every day, but try not to dwell on it. It won't do either of us any good." He held her at arm's length, stressing each word with an element of gravity that frightened her.

"Now listen to me, Kait. I'm going to leave now under the cover of darkness. Wait ten minutes then go back to the Grover mansion." A rare grimness pulled at the corners of his mouth as he studied her reaction. When she started to object, he pressed two fingers to her lips. "Shhh. It has to be this way. We can't take any more chances." A tone of regret crept into his voice.

Their time together had always been so brief, so hurried, but it had been enough for love to grow. She knew in the depths of her soul that they would be together one day for the rest of their lives.

For now that was enough.

Then slowly, almost haltingly, Christopher lowered his mouth to hers. It was a gentle touch with a promise of more to come. Reluctantly, he pulled himself away leaving her with the bittersweet ache of passion unfulfilled once more.

"Now turn around. I can't bear to watch the sadness in those lovely eyes. Humor me, sweet."

She stared at him. "Christopher, I can't." Tears spilled unchecked onto her cheeks.

"Yes you can, my love. Now turn around."

He smiled reassuringly. She thought he must be tapping every bit of strength he could muster to appear calm. They stood quietly, each with a growing awareness of a seemingly impossible dilemma.

Suddenly, the door burst open. Two Confederate soldiers rushed in, pistols raised. Kaitland and Christopher were stunned, silent. Cold fear gripped her, racing down her spine as her mind grappled for a logical reaction that would appear natural. She was, after all, on her own territory.

The soldiers stopped, confusion flickering in their eyes. One of the men stared at Kaitland as recognition dawned. He glanced at Christopher, then shouted without taking his eyes from him.

"Captain, he's in here."

Kaitland heard the rushing footsteps falling on the cobblestone walk. Tim ran through the door. A moment of surprise showed in his eyes, but he seemed to comprehend the situation immediately.

"Good work, Corporal."

"Thank you, sir. I saw the light from under the door. We figured it was a little late for a gunsmith to be working and decided to check it out."

"I should congratulate you, Miss Trevilian. You delayed the escaped prisoner long enough for us to expand the search."

Kaitland held her breath. *Oh Tim*, she cried gratefully

in her heart. Her true relationship with Christopher would be kept a secret among the three of them at least for now if she was to continue her work for the Confederacy. Christopher glanced at her and smiled.

"It was the least I could do, Captain." She moved to stand next to Tim. It was necessary to carry on the charade for the benefit of the enlisted men, but she felt she was deserting Christopher.

"And now, Major or whoever you are, I'm placing you under arrest for espionage. Please turn around." Christopher turned slowly and Tim tied his hands loosely behind his back. "You men find the rest to the search party and tell them we've apprehended the spy."

"Well Captain, here we are again," Christopher said. "I'm sorry to have further spoiled your evening."

"I'll just bet you are. Look, Kaitland told me everything. I don't like this any better than you do, but let's get one thing straight. I'm doing this for her. The only way I could help her is by joining the search in hopes of finding you first. I don't like you and I don't like betraying the Confederacy or my comrades. She's a valuable asset to our cause and—"

"And you're in love with her," Christopher said flatly.

Tim straightened indignantly. His eyes narrowed and bore into Christopher. "That is none of your business, sir."

"Oh, but it is. You see, I love her, too. Do you—"

"Stop it. Just stop it. Both of you," Kaitland shouted, turning her back to the shocked men. She pivoted, greatly angered with them, her slender body stiff with displeasure. She vehemently resented their speaking about her as though she were not there. "How dare you discuss me in such a manner. This is not the time or the place, for heaven's sake. You sound like a couple of school boys." She covered her eyes with her hand and took a deep breath.

"Sorry, Kait. Of course you're right," Tim said. "I wasn't thinking. . ."

"My humble apologies as well." Christopher recognized the stubborn thrust of her lovely jaw and the glint of determination in her eyes.

Sufficiently chastised, the two men looked like little boys who had just received a good scolding. She had to smile. The surreal nature of this entire scenario was almost laughable. The remorse she saw in their faces melted her wrath. "Oh you two. I can't stay angry with either of you."

"I guess we better move out, Donovan." Tim walked toward the door.

"May I have a minute alone with Kait, Captain?"

"You certainly do push your luck." Tim sighed. "All right. One minute. No longer. I'll be right outside."

Christopher turned to meet the apprehension in Kaitland's face. "It's going to be fine, darling. Contrary to his harshness, your friend has a kind heart. He bound my wrists so that freeing my hands shouldn't be difficult. I'll simply wait for the right moment. Now, smile for me, Kait."

She tried, but her eyes pooled with tears. "Why does it have to be this way?"

"Come on, honey, we've beaten the odds twice tonight. Don't give up now. What we've found will last a lifetime. I will come back to you."

"I'll be waiting." There was so much she wanted to say, but time had run out and her emotions were tightening her throat. She only nodded.

"Good. That's my girl. Please be careful, Kait."

In those few parting words she heard love and admiration. Unspoken, she knew, was his fervent wish that she
cease and desist her activities for the Confederacy. It had
become a moot point between them. He accepted the fact
that she was a woman of action, one who was compelled
to follow her conscience.

"Christopher—"

The door swung open. "That's it, Donovan. Let's go."
Tim raised his weapon and pointed it at his prisoner.

"I love you," Christopher whispered, then turned and
walked into the darkness. Tim paused a moment to look at
her, shook his head, and left.

The night grew still once more. She counted herself truly
fortunate that Tim remained such a loyal friend. Despite
the stone that lay heavy in her heart, she knew a brighter
day would dawn.

They had made promises this night, vowing a love that
could not be destroyed by war or separation. She would
keep those thoughts until Christopher's return. In the mean-
time, Glen More was her home and her heritage. Christopher would come for her there. Like the Phoenix bird rising from the ashes, both she and her home would rise above
the destruction of war to create new life and new dreams.
Suddenly, her doubts were gone. She knew those dreams
would be fulfilled when he came back to her.

She raised her head high and with confident steps, walked
out of the shop just as dawn was about to break.

A Letter To Our Readers

Dear Reader:

In order that we might better contribute to your reading enjoyment, we would appreciate your taking a few minutes to respond to the following questions. When completed, please return to the following:

> Rebecca Germany, Editor
> Heartsong Presents
> P.O. Box 719
> Uhrichsville, Ohio 44683

1. Did you enjoy reading *Another Time. . .Another Place*?
   ☐ Very much. I would like to see more books
      by this author!
   ☐ Moderately
      I would have enjoyed it more if _____

   _____

2. Are you a member of *Heartsong Presents*? Yes   No
   If no, where did you purchase this book? _____

   _____

3. What influenced your decision to purchase this
   book? (Check those that apply.)

   ☐ Cover   ☐ Back cover copy

   ☐ Title   ☐ Friends

   ☐ Publicity   ☐ Other _____

4. On a scale from 1 (poor) to 10 (superior), please rate the following elements.

___Heroine   ___Plot

___Hero   ___Inspirational theme

___Setting   ___Secondary characters

5. What settings would you like to see covered in *Heartsong Presents* books?

_____

_____

6. What are some inspirational themes you would like to see treated in future books?_____

_____

_____

7. Would you be interested in reading other *Heartsong Presents* titles?   ❏ Yes   ❏ No

8. Please check your age range:
❏ Under 18   ❏ 18-24   ❏ 25-34
❏ 35-45   ❏ 46-55   ❏ Over 55

9. How many hours per week do you read? ————

Name _____

Occupation _____

Address _____

City _____ State _____ Zip _____

River of Peace
by Janelle Burnham
HP100

A river of grief runs though Ida Thomas.

The remote village of Dawson Creek, British Columbia, has never had a schoolteacher. Since the death of her beloved mother, Ida has never been on her own. Welcomed warmly not only by her students and their families, but the boardinghouse matron as well, Ida feels at home while dealing privately with her pain.

Of all her students Ida finds herself particularly drawn to Ruth McEvan, who is also struggling with a devastating family tragedy. Drawn to Ida, on the other hand, is Ken Danielson, the wealthy son of the local storeowner, who is determined to win the hand of the blond, green-eyed teacher.

While Ida scorns Ken's affections, will she find a man she can truly love, a man to fill her empty heart? Will Ida someday know peace like a river? HP100 $2.95

···· Hearts ♥ong ····

·······`Presents ·······

Heartsong Presents
Love Stories Are Rated G!

That's for godly, gratifying, and of course, great! If you love a thrilling love story, but don't appreciate the sordidness of popular paperback romances, **Heartsong Presents** is for you. In fact, **Heartsong Presents** is the *only inspirational romance book club*, the only one featuring love stories where Christian faith is the primary ingredient in a marriage relationship.

Sign up today to receive your first set of four, never before published Christian romances. Send no money now; you will receive a bill with the first shipment. You may cancel at any time without obligation, and if you aren't completely satisfied with any selection, you may return the books for an immediate refund!

Imagine. . .four new romances every month—two historical, two contemporary—with men and women like you who long to meet the one God has chosen as the love of their lives. . .all for the low price of $9.97 postpaid.

To join, simply complete the coupon below and mail to the address provided. **Heartsong Presents** romances are rated G for another reason: They'll arrive *Godspeed!*
